TODAY
TOMORROW
AND
FOREVER

TODAY
TOMORROW
AND
FOREVER

THE PREQUEL TO
ETERNAL FLAME

PATRICIA GARBER

DEDICATION:

*To the biggest Elvis fan I know, my husband,
Daniel Wayne Hawthorne!
I love you so much, honey.*

SPECIAL THANKS:

*To Tammy Powers Billingsley, who so creatively titled
this book—thank you for your insights and friendship.
Today, Tomorrow and Forever was a great choice.*

CHAPTER ONE

(The Angel)

"He will command his angels concerning you to guard you carefully."

— Luke 4:10

Demons. Their presence permeated the air with a lingering, putrid stench. How does something of the spirit emit a decomposition-like odor yet remain undetected by the living? If he hadn't seen it, he wouldn't have believed it. Then again, he was no longer among the living.

Lifting his chin, he gave the equivalent of a physical inhale. *Three,* he considered. *Maybe four.* Why were there so many demons? Was the threat significant enough to warrant this small army? He didn't want to look, but it was his post, so he glanced at the angulating mass in the corner.

"Ugly sons of Bs," he muttered before his attention snapped to the four living souls seated around a desk at the center of the room. *They're scared*. He could smell that, too.

Fear smelled sweet and sour, like a room full of tainted cotton candy. If he'd been in the flesh rather than the spirit, the mixture would have turned his stomach. Yet, beyond the suffering, something else had attracted these demons like a child irresistibly drawn to the excitement of a town fair. That irresistible ingredient now hovered over one living soul in the room.

Mrs. Bennett, child of God, wife to a local Atlanta pastor, and most importantly, mother to his assigned human, Samantha Lynn Bennett, sat in the middle chair, her legs crossed at the ankles. Although she appeared calm on the surface, her black patent pumps bounced with nervous energy. Pale and thin, she dressed impeccably in dark blue jeans, a loose, white silk blouse, and a blue scarf around her neck. His top lip curled into a Cheshire grin. Yeah, his lip still did that.

Turning, he considered how Samantha, seated to her mother's right, was a true reflection of her mother's southern gentility. Wearing a dark navy stew uniform, or more appropriately stated for the times, inflight safety personnel attire, Samantha fiddled with the edges of the skirt stretched tight across her knees. Mrs. Bennett reached for Samantha's hand as Pastor Bennett, Sam's father, sat rod-iron straight on his wife's left. Even from across the room, he could see sweat dripping down the pastor's forehead, soaking into the collar of his bleached white shirt.

When a demon in the corner hissed, his attention snapped to the grumbling abomination. He snarled, daring it to make his day. The writhing mass fell still, and just because he could, he issued an order.

"That's right, spawn of Satan, shut your trap."

The evil horde quivered, not from fear. No, it would need a sense of self-preservation to suffer fear. From experience, he'd say these monsters were more reactive, like a snake stalking prey in high grass.

Its outline glowed red, pulsating with what one might call rage—or was that excitement? While this demon dance was concerning, he needed to understand its attendance, so he began to taunt the unwanted guests. "Is it hot in hell, fellas? Do y'all need a vacation?"

A bony appendage jetted from its mass, spindly fingers reaching out to the world, wrist twisting unnaturally until four skeletal digits curled inward, executing a crude middle finger salute.

"Well, all be…did you just shoot me the bird?" He chuckled, and the mass bounced as if filled with joy. He understood that cheerful demons were a contradiction, and he was about to offer some rather un-Christian advice when a metal chair scraped against the clinic floor.

Turning, he saw Samantha, his assigned responsibility, staring at the same dark corner. His attention was fixed on her bewildered expression. Those familiar sky-blue eyes were now slate grey, and her once caramel complexion turned pale ivory. The mother beside her reached over and took Sam's hand, pulling her attention back to the doctor seated at the large, mahogany desk, where scientific words like *metastasized* echoed in the air.

Mrs. Bennett smiled, mouthing a faint, "We're going to be okay."

Sam's lips twitched as her gaze shifted to the dark corner, lingering there while the demon twisted with collective impatience.

I sure didn't see that coming, he thought. And the demon in the corner grumbled as if it, too, found this development curious. As if heaven and hell gave pause, the room went stale as all spiritual quintessence's held their imaginary breaths. *How did I miss this?*

He ran the mystery through every known calculation, from coincidence to a blessed talent; it felt impossible that he'd miss something this big. He had been Sam's guardian angel since she'd come to faith, which was young because she was a pastor's kid. And in all that time—nearly 23 years—Sam had never displayed *the gift*.

Then again, maybe this wasn't so surprising?

He chuckled when remembering the six-year-old as if it were yesterday—long, chestnut-colored curls like her mother's, dimples as big as Texas, and a stubbornness that had, unfortunately for all, followed her into adulthood. Samantha was such a quiet yet strong-willed little girl, and now, at twenty-seven, she was much the same—only taller!

Cancer. He heard the doctor think the diagnosis only seconds before he spoke the words, like dropping a grenade into the room. The family, his first of many guardian assignments, became perfectly still. Heartbeats plummeted in unison, but tears streamed down Sam's face first. Though angels don't cry while in spirit, he could still feel their collective emotion—terror and overwhelming sadness, their heads full of questions. Samantha's father fell into a silent, desperate prayer.

My God, Father almighty. Please calm this storm. The prayer repeated in Pastor Bennett's mind like a record needle stuck in a deep groove. *Take away this cup. Please, Lord, take it away!*

As these prayers went straight to heaven, his concern returned to Mrs. Bennett, now frozen in her chair. Strands of emotionally charged energy sparked around her. The fireworks of colors were beautiful as her aura flashed from blue to red and back again. The demons in the corner morphed, and again, bony hands reached out, clawing and grasping, desperate for a taste of her grief.

Mrs. Bennett didn't move. Not a twitch of her foot. No wringing of hands. Nothing. *Was she even blinking?* Though standing behind her, he could see slight shoulders gently moving up and down with each surprisingly steady breath. Had he been able, he would have moved to console her, instantly absorbing the family's anxiety deep within his soul.

Throughout his life, he was a man of action who took responsibility for and cared for many people. His tour schedule was proof of how far he'd go to provide for those he loved, performing a rigorous 295 days a year, often two shows a day. From his mother and father to a wife and daughter and a host of cousins and friends, he devoted himself wholeheartedly and worked himself into an early grave. Looking back, he'd do it all over again. He liked caring for those he loved because he loved deeply, and when love runs that deep, you give of yourself up to that last drawn breath.

As he watched Sam embracing her mother, he felt like a benched football player who's been training for years and is ready to run the winning touchdown. But the coach, the big guy upstairs, had not called him in… not yet. *And what about those demons?* He glanced back to the corner, where the black mass was back to dancing as if joyfulness was even possible for angels of hell. *Were they also waiting on orders?*

There was a time when he waited on no one. Everything he desired was at his fingertips. The world bent to his every need because he was the heartthrob of a generation, a singer-entertainer known worldwide by just one name. But this wasn't a stage. And the demons in the corner weren't in one of his movies. This was real. And they wanted Samantha Lynn Bennett. His Sam. Who was placed in his care, twenty-three years, four days, and two months after his own death on August 16th, 1977.

From the headlines that read, "Elvis Presley Dead at 42," to this exact moment, he had known his heavenly purpose. And as he released his wings—yes, angels really do have wings—and with a six-foot reach on either side, layer after layer of fluttering power, he shot an admittedly cocky smirk towards the dark mass in the corner.

"Get ready, jackasses," he hissed. "It's taking care of business time!"

CHAPTER TWO

(Samantha)

"I am sending an angel ahead of you to guard you along the way and bring you to the place I have prepared."

— EXODUS 23:20

(Eight hours earlier)

My cell phone was already ringing when we landed at Atlanta International Airport, the name 'Daddy' insistently flashing as Captain Jackson slammed on the airplane's brakes. Outside the plane's portal window, thick landing tires ploughed through melted puddles of ice, and my buttocks slid forward in the flight-crew seat. A second later, someone's cell phone chimed with a Christmas jingle— 'Rudolph the Red-Nosed Reindeer'. I rolled my eyes at Heather, my best friend and number two crew member on this hideous flight from Dallas to Atlanta.

"The captain did that on purpose, you know that, right?" Heather hissed under her breath, careful not to criticize while around customers. I nodded my agreement.

Typically, the first officers made the landings, as most captains allowed their counterparts to gain more hours for their advancement. However, Captain Jackson was different; he was far too egocentric for that. When the seatbelt sign dinged, Heather and I quickly stood up in unison with the passengers to collect our crew bags. Captain Jackson's voice screeched through the airplane's hull as I marveled at the mathematical miracle of how his head had managed to fit inside the small cockpit of this Boeing 737.

"How about that landing, girls?" the grey-haired man looking like ole Saint Nick in a black flight uniform asked with a smirk before adding, "That'll tone them buttocks!"

Everyone except Heather fake laughed. Now that all customers had deplaned, I braced for the retort I knew would come.

"You think our butts need tightening, do you, Captain?" Heather asked, and twisted to look Captain Jackson square in the eye, then bent over. "What do you think, Sam, how's my ass?"

Here we go, I thought, barely able to utter anything but a, "Uh, well…" And because I was terrible at coed sparring games, I just shut my mouth.

"I'm sure human resources would love to know about these workouts, don't you think, sir?" Heather continued, pushing a blonde strand of hair behind her ear while invisible daggers chased the captain as he attempted to exit.

But he had only managed two steps off the airplane when Heather's words sank in. He turned slowly, a cold wind blowing through the jet bridge and tossing his red snowman tie as anger flashed across his face. Meanwhile, the first officer continued walking, seemingly unfazed; clearly, this wasn't his first inappropriate rodeo.

While my instinct was to run from the conflict, I stood behind my friend. In fact, unbeknown to me, two other crew members were standing in form over my shoulder, which made four females in total. And when Jackson looked upon this united front, his steely, grey-blue eyes squinted with a challenge.

I didn't have to look to know we were all smiling. I'd like to think my grin was pure defiance, but I was nervous and, somewhere deep down, secretly hoping my dimples, a gift from my mother, might disarm him. But the captain didn't seem to notice our smiles. He was laser-focused on Heather.

"We're a whole day late, Captain," Heather volleyed, striking points for us all.

Point. Game. Set.

While in Jackson Hole, good ole Jackson had complained that the Velcro cover on his seat kept slipping, thus causing significant discomfort to his delicate derriere. He couldn't fly three hours like that, now, could he? And because Wyoming was a small station, they'd had no immediate answer to the fix, and thus, we were all sent to a local hotel to wait out the repair.

"Fatigue is a real safety concern," the captain quipped, and with a single finger, he pushed his winged hat back like in an old western.

"Did he just compare his buttocks to a safety issue?" I whispered to Heather, leaning in closer as if to improve my hearing.

We stood at an impasse, four pairs of black pumps firmly pressed on the carpet. With Heather's blonde hair catching the wintery breeze like in a superhero movie, we were poised for battle. Behind me, I could hear the other women giggling. Captain Jackson shook his head as if calculating the risk and not liking the odds.

"I see you all have lost your sense of humor today." Jackson expelled a dramatic sigh before he turned to leave, and we waited a beat before following.

With our exit in sight, we passed a grinning gate agent, and I resisted the urge to offer her an untouched bag of popcorn because popcorn should come with every sideshow.

"Can't fly with them, can't eject them at thirty thousand feet," Heather said as she passed the watchful gate agent, who I imagined exhaled a breath of relief.

While the three-day trip with Captain Bighead had failed to lift my spirits, the missed call and my family's awaited appointment consumed my thoughts even more.

"I'm sorry this trip was so bad." I reached for Heather, aware that our after-trip dinner routine would have to wait. "But I need to get to the hospital."

"Oh, that's right," she cooed, jumping into my embrace. "Give your momma a hug for me."

As I rushed to catch the employee bus, shielding my eyes from the glare of the winter sun, I recalled something my father always said: "Life is what's happening while you're on a trip." He was right. My dream of working for an airline wasn't everything I'd imagined. While it was exciting to visit new and unseen places at every stop, it was demanding—

a 24/7 commitment, 360 days a year. That meant a lot of missed Sundays and holidays.

"I'm just getting to my car, Daddy. I'll be there soon." While fumbling for my car keys, I left my father a voicemail, ending with the response that I knew would ease his concerns, "Don't worry, I won't speed. Love you both."

The hospital was 15 miles away and traffic was lighter than expected for Atlanta at nine o'clock in the morning. With the rush hour crunch over and the lunch crowd still several hours away, I chose the freeway and set my BMW's cruise to 65. As the sun radiated through the car's window, warming my cold and tense muscles, I flipped on the radio and set it to a local station. Instantly, a man's voice blared, and I heard something about a shooting downtown.

Some family is minus a loved one this Christmas, I thought, sadness rising in my chest.

Quickly, I flipped the car's stereo to Bluetooth. The center console flashed, and the screen highlighted a playlist titled 'Hunk of A Man'. I tapped it and Elvis's smooth baritone flowed from the speakers, my grip loosening around the car's steering wheel.

"Forever, my darling," I sang along, rolling my shoulders while admiring the streetlights decorated in holiday greenery, complete with red Christmas bows.

Hospital, second exit, a sign up ahead said, and as I was merging into the lane, my cell phone rang. "I'm almost there," I said into the car's speakers.

"Hey, girl, sorry to interrupt," Heather's voice echoed. "I wanted to apologize again."

The sound of her soft Alabama drawl told me she was back to her ordinarily level-headed self. "It's okay, really. I understand."

"That Jackson just burns me!"

"He does me, too."

"I won't keep you. Give me a call when you can." Heather let out a sigh and then, in her typical style, hung up without waiting for a reply.

The sound of love in her words flooded my eyes, drawing further attention to the deep wounds surrounding my heart. For four months, I've struggled with the gut-wrenching grief felt when one watches a loved one in pain. Often, I would check on Mother only to find her delicate frame sitting at the bedroom vanity, staring at herself in the mirror. Those green eyes that had mothered me through many childhood illnesses looked at me in a state of confusion.

"Baby girl, why do you suppose that's happening?" she'd ask, pointing to the whites of her eyes, more yellow than the day before.

A feeling of helplessness washed over me. No one had the answer—not my daddy, not the church congregation who loved and prayed for my mother. Not even the doctors who could treat the pain but were unable to find the source. With only two weeks left before Christmas, many unanswered questions were about to be revealed.

As I drove in the warmth of my car, I still felt a shiver from the countless hours I had spent searching on Google, which had left me dreading today. "Hey, Google, what organ is found here?" and "Google, what if said organ hurts?" Note to self: if you can't handle Ask Google, it is best not to ask Google questions. If one must, then be warned of the bottomless rabbit hole that awaits, inspiring one to search into the wee hours of the morning to no avail.

Once parked on level four of the Atlanta Hospital, I began shedding the uniform I'd been wearing since three o'clock that morning in Dallas. Removing my jacket's visible name tags, I rolled up the sleeves of the white, company-issued shirt. Finally stepping out, I paused to consider my reflection in the car's side window.

"More casual," I coached. "And less worry."

Mother's doctor was in suite 204, and I went straight to it because I'd taken her to a few appointments, so I knew where it was already. The heavy door creaked on its hinges, alerting the grandmotherly receptionist at her desk inside.

"Hello, dear." She spoke with a friendly but authoritative tone. "Go on back. They're waiting for you. First room on the right."

My stomach dropped like an air pocket at thirty thousand feet. And in that moment, I did what I always do in the air. I clenched everything—my jaw, fist, stomach muscles...even my glute muscles were tight! *Darn that Captain Jackson!*

"Well, go on now, don't make your momma wait." The receptionist's reprimand urged me through one door and then another without knocking.

When the door to the private room opened, my gaze immediately landed on my mother. Always the optimist, she smiled at me. Whatever it was that gave her courage—perhaps her faith in God—she was steadfast in her resolve. Throughout my life, she had always been our family's calm leader, no matter the problem at hand. In that moment, she appeared as serene as ever, dressed casually yet stylish, her cheeks rosy as if she'd just come in from tending to her rose garden.

Daddy, on the other hand, looked a mess! His light blue eyes were red from what I assumed was a lack of sleep. And as he sat next to Mother, one hand clutching a bible, his silver-fox hair standing up on its ends, a worry for his wellbeing grew in my stomach. I'd never seen him look so disheveled. If how I felt was any indication of how I looked, we were likely two peas in the same messy pod. The thought made me smirk, but when he looked my way, the watery emotions I saw in his eyes caused that half smile to instantly drop away.

"Come here, baby girl," Mother said, motioning for me to take the empty seat to her right. As I did, I kissed her cheek lightly, leaning over to take my father's hand and squeeze it before being seated.

The room felt cold. And I don't mean the circumstance made it chilly, though there was that—it was downright freezing. Goosebumps instantly crawled up my arms and over my neck. As I tugged at my uniform skirt, trying to coax it closer to my shaking knees, I reflected on the jacket I'd left in the car with longing.

"Thank you for coming, Samantha," Doctor Nguyen began. "What we need to discuss is going to affect the entire family. Your father and mother felt it best that we talk here."

I weighed up his words, hearing, 'Something bad is coming', and instantly squirmed. Mother took my hand, interrupting my nervous habit of fiddling with my attire. Her touch allowed me to release a breath that, until that moment, I was unaware I'd been holding.

I glanced over at Mother and caught a quick movement out of the corner of my eye. It happened so fast—just a flash or a spark of something black and white. In those brief seconds, I realized that the colors weren't just one; they were side by side, made up of many shades. Whatever I saw was so fleeting that if I'd blinked, I would have missed it entirely.

"Cancer?" My mother's words were almost a whimper, pulling me back to the moment. "Pancreatic. Are you sure?"

The diagnosis all but jumped into the room, like hot garbage emanating an odor from nowhere and everywhere, all at once. I groaned as my stomach wrenched, lurching forward to hold a hand to my mouth. My parents looked on with concern as I scanned every corner of the room, noting the sound of a floor vent rattling near my feet. Then, a cool breeze rushed up my skirt; everything about this moment felt wrong. And while my senses were preoccupied, my mother retook my hand.

"It's going to be alright." Her calm nature would have settled me if not for the reflection of light I could see pulsating behind her, like a wrinkle in time and space.

While it flexed in colorful strands, a single tear fell hot down my cheek. Next to me, my father's eyes were closed, and I knew he was praying. Daddy's first reflexive response was always set to God. My first reaction was, as usual, useless. I didn't move. And even in stillness, I shamefully wondered, am I a bad daughter? Is Daddy a lousy husband?

Why are we being punished?

"Doctor," I huffed, voice gurgling from tears, "are you sure?"

"It was just a backache," my father explained. His voice sounded small like he was muttering in the wind.

"I'm sorry, Mrs. Bennett." The doctor's jet-black eyes settled on my mother. "There are treatments we can discuss. They may prolong your life for a time, but you are now in stage four. That's one year with treatment, three to six months without. "

"No, that's not right." I shook my head. "Look again, Doctor, please look again."

"It was just a damn backache!" Daddy's emotions crashed through the room.

"Richard." Mama reached for my father's arm with her free hand and held it tight.

"We need a second opinion," I said to anyone listening, hanging on one rational thought like it was the only life vest in a sinking boat. Daddy grunted his approval.

"No," Momma quickly interrupted.

Daddy and I whipped her way so fast that a neck muscle twanged down my collarbone. It wasn't only pain that held my tongue. My mother's green eyes flashed, radiating with a familiar impatience. The kind that said this wasn't up for debate.

"Doctor, we thank you for your time," my mother said matter-of-factly and began to gather her purse. "We're going home."

The monarch had spoken.

CHAPTER THREE

(The Angel)

"My God sent his angel and shut the lion's mouth."
— DANIEL 6:22

The Bennett household was dimly lit. A late evening sun filtered through wooden window shades, casting a narrow beam of light across the flocked Christmas tree in the corner. A black and white tuxedo cat observed as Elvis sat on the couch, dressed entirely in white, praying and waiting.

"Boo!" He smirked, and the animal hissed back.

He was trying to remember the cat's name—Boop or Bob? —when he heard Samantha's silver BMW pull into the driveway, followed by the Bennetts's Cadillac.

A moment later, a collection of doors slammed, and footsteps approached. The cat stood and Elvis sat up straighter.

When the front door swung open, a chilly breeze rushed in, followed by Mrs. Bennett, the pastor, and then Samantha. Although a shared sorrow lingered among them, he felt relieved to see no demons had followed them inside.

Did they heed his warning? he wondered, though that seemed unlikely.

Nobody spoke. The silence amongst the living was like an unhappy guest at a party, longing to leave but refusing to go.

"Hey, Boots buddy," Sam spoke first, picking up the black and white cat and gathering the furry animal to her chest while sitting in the nearest armchair.

Boots! He remembered with a smile. Shortened from Bootsy to Boots after the realization that the abandoned kitten wasn't female.

The feline squirmed before eventually settling on Samantha's lap. Its yellow eyes seemed to be judging him or perhaps gloating from a distance—he wasn't quite sure. However, if he hadn't known better, he would have thought the cat enjoyed being the only living creature privy to his presence. Fortunately, Boots soon grew bored, and like all cats do, fell asleep in the warmth of a loving companion's lap.

"We need a second opinion," Pastor Bennett said while taking a seat on the couch next to him. Though it wasn't necessary, Elvis shifted over and gave the worried father some room.

"Right," Sam agreed.

Grief is difficult to witness, even for angels. The struggles of humankind remind us of our own human experience. Nothing reflects the fear of the unknown quite like death—the threat of it, the act of dying, the hope of reprieve all inspire the living to examine their lives more closely. That's exactly what Mrs. Bennett was doing—evaluating her life and contemplating her next move. He could hear her talking to God from the kitchen, where she busily rummaged through the cabinets. What was she looking for? He didn't know.

I don't want to die, Lord. But if this is your will, I'm ready. Her mind fought with her heart. *But my family is not prepared.*

"Honey," the pastor said, "what do you think? Sam and I agree, we need a second opinion."

When Mrs. Bennett entered the living room, she held a teapot and three cups. There was a look of determination and acceptance in her eyes, and he could sense the fight and exhaustion flowing through her like a wave from the ocean. Wanting to help and aware that a calm atmosphere was needed, he closed his eyes, reached deep within himself, and radiated a green light. When he opened his eyes again, the rays formed a halo that filled the living room, spreading throughout the space, illuminating the corners and climbing the walls. He smiled, aware that balance and harmony were essential as a difficult conversation was about to take place.

From Samantha's lap, the napping cat stirred. Boots lifted his head and perked up his ears. As he watched the glittery streaks, his pupils dilated from yellow to nearly black, signaling his growing interest. Then, as if seeking confirmation, he looked back at Elvis, who smiled at him. While the high emotions in the room settled, the cat resumed his nap—clearly unimpressed.

Tough audience. He chuckled.

"You know, Richard," Mrs. Bennett spoke as she filled the family's cups with steaming tea, adding sugar and cream to her husband's beverage first, "I don't want to waste whatever time I have."

"What do you mean, Mom?" Sam asked before the pastor could respond to his wife's admission.

"I mean, honey," Mrs. Bennett said, glancing at her daughter, sliding Samantha a cup before taking a seat in a recliner opposite them all, "you're too young to understand, but time is precious, and I'm going to enjoy it without restrictions."

"You're not going to fight?" Sam's voice escalated as disbelief and shock gripped her.

"That's not what she's saying," the pastor muttered.

"That is what she's saying, Daddy!"

"Honey, tell her that's not what you're saying."

Mrs. Bennett calmly picked up her cup and took a sip. The room went still, all eyes focused on the one with the final say. "But that is what I'm saying, Richard."

He averted his eyes as Samantha and her father went pale, mouths hanging open.

"Momma!" Sam's disappointed tone tugged at his heart.

From the corner of his eye, he noticed that Boots was making a break for it. The little cat's four white feet moved quickly down the hall, with its tail held straight out for balance. *Poor little guy,* he thought, before closing his eyes and pushing a blue light of energy around every living soul in the room. The calming color enveloped the space, pulsating a radiant sense of peace.

"Sam..." The pastor raised his hands, palms out. "Let your mother explain."

The room fell still as a setting sun filtered through the blinds, its rays overcoming the darkness to cast a glow of hope.

"I'm going to pray on it." Mrs. Bennett cleared her throat, pushing a strand of long, brunette hair away from her face, before addressing Sam directly. "It's stage four, honey."

"I know, but—"

"Sam!" Mrs. Bennett's voice boomed, and Elvis's eyes shifted to his white boots as he tried to remember if he'd ever heard the gentle woman raise her voice. "Do you think I want to die?"

Despite the still-throbbing energy lights, the pastor's tears continued to flow, a testament to his profound struggle. A wave of helplessness engulfed him, and he bowed his head as Elvis resumed his prayers.

The most challenging part of any angelic mission was witnessing human suffering, knowing that divine intervention is possible but not permitted. Both humans and angels are bound by the unfathomable mystery of God. The knowledge that a mere nod from above could end this suffering was almost too much for him to bear. He grappled with the righteousness of it all, understanding that the integrity of God's relationship with man must be upheld, even in the face of injustice.

"I think we'll pray on it." The pastor's voice was diminished, nothing like his typical Sunday morning boom. "Let's take it to the church congregation. Let them pray on it too."

Samantha rolled her eyes. While a single tear trickled down her cheek, Elvis reflected on a younger Sam. He remembered this childlike behavior well. It was a common sight when she was eight and didn't get her way—but now? Stress. But mostly grief.

"It's been a long day." Mrs. Bennett stood, her hand quickly shifting to her back for needed support. "Let's get some rest and revisit this in the morning."

All watched as the mother of one slowly took her exit, weariness weighing down her shoulders, footsteps heavy as she trudged down the hall to the bedroom in the back. The scene brought back a memory, one of his own momma; her worries while on earth were many, and like Mrs. Bennett, she too relied on her faith for comfort.

"That's just great," Sam growled, clearly still in anger mode. But the pastor wasn't listening, his gaze focused on the site of Mrs. Bennett's exit. "Now what?"

He let out a sigh and once again, the pastor didn't answer; he merely got up and followed his wife.

"Fine." Sam slapped a palm on the couch cushion at her side. "Let's all just go to bed."

The next few minutes were marked by the clock ticking from across the room. The glow of blue and green energy continued to flare, and while he and Boots were the only ones who could see it, the colors were comforting. Doubt crept into his mind, questioning whether his presence today had even helped. It was then that Mr. Boots reappeared, eyes glowing in the dark. The cat paused, considering him before leaping back into Samantha's lap.

"Hey, Bootsy," she cooed. "Did we scare you?" The cat pressed its head to her chest, the rumbling sound of purring echoing through the room.

As Boots reveled in the attention, Elvis considered the woman across from him. She'd come so far. That small kid with freckles and ringlets had grown into the beautiful woman before him. Even in the low light, her delicate frame emanated an elegance and fragility that any man or angel would want to protect.

Although he'd always had a weakness for pretty women, he questioned whether his attachment to Sam was a good enough reason for God to deny him the flesh. While angels are servants, they must be careful when asked to walk amongst humans. The flesh is weak, and one does not want to fall into the same trap as Satan, who, once the most beautiful Angel, soon believed he, too, should be worshiped. Since the world and Elvis had a bond—rock star and all—he wondered whether God worried that he was not strong enough to endure the flesh.

"We'll sleep here," said Sam, stroking the cat while she talked. "No point in dirtying the bedsheets, right, Mr. Big Boots?"

Samantha's conversation with Mr. Big Boots—catchy nickname—intruded on his thoughts as he watched her settle in for the night. He observed her shifting the couch pillows and carefully unfolding a blanket, ensuring every fold and tuck was perfect. He considered her anxiety, hoping it wouldn't trigger a night-walking episode. Although she hadn't sleepwalked since childhood, he understood how waking up in an unfamiliar place could heighten her stress. He winced at the memory of a time he had sleepwalked out into the streets of Tupelo, which had given his mother quite a scare. As he reminisced, Samantha kicked off her work shoes and began to untuck her uniform blouse. He looked away when she unzipped her skirt.

Privacy was a God-given right to all!

As a soft light filtered into the living room, he decided it was safe to look. With great curiosity, he observed Samantha fiddling with an object in her hand. He recognized it as a smaller version of a car phone, like a crude model he'd had in his day. The tapping and sliding he'd witnessed suggested it captured her full attention. When she gave it a single tap, music flowed from the device, filling the room with a song he recognized.

"Dang it," Sam said, fumbling with the phone until the volume lowered. He looked away with a smirk.

The music was pleasant, romantic even. The rich tone elevated the moment until he found himself rocking to the rhythm of his own voice, the chords soothing to even an angel. And when Samantha began to mindlessly sing along, he couldn't help but smile.

That's my girl, he thought. *Can't carry a note and doesn't care!*

Reclining in a chair across the room, Elvis watched the day's grief set in. Her normally soft features tightened with worry, creating hard lines on her forehead. Her eyes, usually bright and full of life, now carried a weight he could feel. When she pulled out a leather-bound paisley journal from her purse, he stood up and moved to her side.

Samantha had been journaling her whole life, and it was a good thing, as it was a way for him to understand her every emotion, from her heart to her mind. Initially, he felt a sting of guilt whenever he watched her write, telling himself that this was another moment of privacy he should respect. However, he recognized her journaling as a gift, especially since her body and soul were in his care.

Pastor Bennett had started his daughter's journaling habit. *I should really thank him*, Elvis thought, because by teaching his daughter how to communicate with God outside of prayer, it had become a fundamental way for him to keep her safe. Even angels find their adolescent responsibilities challenging, a teenager's moods are ever-changing. They often jump from one topic to another and express a wide range of emotions, from everyday feelings to more serious ones. There is much to say about the insights that can be gained from the gift of writing.

For example, when Samantha had a crush on a young man in high school... What was his name? Jimmy. That was it. And Jimmy, though not a bad kid, had some rough-and-tumble friends. Jimmy was in a rock and roll band—yeah, he knew that sounded hypocritical. But it wasn't Jimmy he was worried about. It was John, the bass player. And where Jimmy went, so did John. Long story short, Samantha's journaling had clued him into her intentions of sneaking out with the boys in the band one summer, which allowed him time to influence Pastor Bennett and see that those plans never took action.

Good thing, too, as the car accident that happened that night due to underage drinking would have had Samantha in the wrong place at the wrong time. Though Jimmy was unhurt, he couldn't say the same for John, who spent his entire senior year in physical rehabilitation. After that, Mr. Bennett prohibited Samantha from hanging out with Jimmy and the band. Which suited Elvis just fine.

As he watched Samantha begin to journal that night, he felt no guilt as he read her words. There was concern and love mixed with a pang of sadness. He knew there was no way to remove the cup she would be forced to endure. If there had been, he would gladly have done so.

December 11th

Dear God, it's me, Sam.

I'm at a loss for words, so forgive me if this entry is rude. But, seriously, what in the name of J.C. are you doing? It's almost Christmas, and my mother has cancer? And not only does she have it, but she's in stage four? Stage four of an untreatable cancer... Have you lost your heart, your mind, and all that is holy and just? My mother, the one who praises you every day, is dying! In fact, I'd be willing to bet that while I'm out here complaining and being disrespectful, she's kneeling by her bed and praying right now! Does that seem fair? You're going to fix this, right? You're going to wave a magic wand, move a mountain, or drain the very sea to help her?

Please, help her.

Samantha's pen was swift, and he struggled to keep up, distracted by an uneasy shift in the room temperature from warm to cool. Sam was so focused she didn't see her own breath, and he didn't have to look to know the corners were darker, denser than before. Though nothing would appear visible to the naked eye, evil always watches from the depths of hell. They feed on emotions like anger, which can call a horde of demons as quickly as horses to the barn at feeding time.

Now, extra cautious, he kept one eye on the dark shadows. As he asked himself whether he was overreacting, he glanced back just in time to read Samantha's last words.

I promise you. If you do nothing, and she dies...I'm done with you!

If he'd had a physical heart, it would have indeed stopped...for the second time in his existence!

CHAPTER FOUR

(Samantha)

"The angel of the Lord encamps around those who fear him, and He delivers them."

— Psalm 34:7

My cell phone pinged at 5:00 the next morning. I grunted, cursing the nudge that dared to wake me. While I squinted in the early glow, the phone chimed again. I pulled it out from under my pillow but didn't immediately look at it.

The day could wait, I thought. And the cat seemed to agree as Mr. Boots pushed himself up at my side, eyes half shut, performing a full body stretch. The sight looked so good that I found myself envying the cat.

"I bet that feels fabulous," I cooed. Stroking the feline's long, grey fur, I swooped a hand down Boot's spine and up his tail. He arched into my touch. "Can we switch places for the day? You be the human and I'll be the cat?"

As if in response, Boots pressed his head to my cheek, lifting his chin in one comforting stroke. Tiny whiskers tickled my nose as he purred in my face, that rumbling, slight engine-like sound of a cat's approval.

Finally turning my phone over, the screen illuminated, and a missed call flashed a familiar number—inflight crew scheduling. The department handling crew schedules often called with extra flying options or sick call repositioning requests. But I hadn't put in to fly extra this month, so I groaned over the knowledge that it had to be the latter; someone was sick, and I was next on the list to fill in.

"Great," I quietly huffed, my mind racing over the options: call back but decline or call out sick and take the attendance strike? Or admit the tragedy that is my life and beg for leniency? But duty called, and I knew I had to respond.

They may allow me a reprieve. The thought made me laugh. My first for the day.

From deep in the house, I heard the distant sound of a toilet flushing as I punched the voicemail codes to listen to the news I knew was coming.

"Good morning, Ms. Bennett. This is Tracie from crew scheduling. We have a sick call on a JFK turn this morning. Please call back within the hour. Sign-in is at 9:00 a.m."

I turned my wrist over and registered that it was now 5:30 a.m. At least I'd been given my required union notice, but I'd still need to get home to shower and change. Though it was only one flight down and back, the idea of leaving weighed heavy.

Can I perform my duties professionally? I wondered. My emotions were a turbulent sea, but I knew I had to navigate them to focus on work.

"What are you doing awake, baby girl?" My father's voice floated into the room. When I turned, he was paused at the kitchen entrance, bible in hand and waiting for a response.

"Flight scheduling called." I held up my mobile phone with a frown.

"Awe, coffee it is then," he said before slipping out of sight into the kitchen.

A moment later, the kitchen light flickered on, and I squinted at the intrusive brilliance as every muscle in my body begged for sleep. Flopping back onto the couch, I stared at the ceiling and the specks of glittered plaster I remembered as a child. Countless times, I'd lain here, struggling with the day's choices. For example, would I accept Jimmy's invitation to prom? Would it be college after graduation, as Daddy wanted? Or should I chase dreams and head for the flight academy in Los Angeles?

"Cream?" Daddy asked from the kitchen, reminding me it's not polite to ignore the house host. Although this was my childhood home, and the room down the hall had been mine for 18 years, good manners dictated the adult in me to get up and offer a hand.

"Don't you have to call them back?" Daddy asked as I entered the kitchen, taking a seat at the round table in the corner.

A closed bible lay on the table across from me. Why did it seem like God was always close but unwilling? When it came to God's help, Daddy preached that the Almighty's timing was not our own. Now, squinting at it, I tried to judge whether it was friend or foe this time.

"I have an hour to return the call," I explained, taking a seat and wincing over the feel of the cold wood against my bottom. "I'm not sure I'm going to accept the reassignment."

"Do you have a choice?"

"Yes and no." I considered whether revealing the list of excuses already spinning inside my head would be worth a speech about honesty. "It's only a turn, New York and back, but I don't want to leave, Daddy, not now."

Daddy thought about that for a moment. Then, with a sigh, he simply said, "I'll be okay," before lifting the coffee cup for that first taste, undoubtedly the best part of any morning. "Besides, I have a meeting at the church that I cannot miss."

"Life pauses for no man?" I quoted my father's words, but he only grunted in agreement. "And what about Momma?"

"Your mother's sleeping." He turned, placing sugar and cream on the table. "She'll be there for a while yet, I imagine."

When Daddy placed a small cup on the table, the smell of roasted coffee beans encircled us, and whether it was conditional or environmental, my once-tense shoulder muscles instantly relaxed. Reminiscing on how I'd missed these early morning coffee chats with my father, I gave a light chuckle.

"What's so funny?"

"I was thinking of when I moved back to Atlanta last year." I paused as my father sat across from me. "Well, this wasn't exactly how I thought it would go."

He didn't say a word. It may have been the first time I'd seen my father speechless.

"I better get going," I said, pushing the coffee cup away. "I'll need to get showered and find a clean uniform before I head to the airport."

"Will you return later?" My father's sky-blue eyes pleaded. No doubt, he did not want to suffer this day alone.

"Yes," I said softly, rising to my feet and stretching to kiss his cheek. "I'll see you for dinner."

As I grabbed my purse from the couch, collecting my cell phone and discarded uniform items, I felt a tug down the hallway of my childhood home. My parents' room had been right across from my own, and I stared at the doorway to where my mother now napped.

How can this be happening to us, to my family? My mother loved God, and my parents had dedicated their lives to Him and His message! Why would God allow this to happen? The questions re-sparked the deep anger from the night before, reminding me of the words I'd put to paper.

If you do nothing, and she dies...I'm done with you!

I had meant it. But the knowledge that it was only a few short hours ago when I'd given God an ultimatum shamed me. The memory clawed at my soul. It ran side by side with all that now threatened my future, shredding my peace of mind. Destroying any chance for happiness.

My roots were deeply embedded in the church, nurtured by Sunday school and the guidance of Mrs. Madeline Rudabaker, or Maddy, as I fondly called her. I respected the faith my parents had instilled in me, but a lingering question tormented me. Had I somehow brought God's wrath upon my family? I couldn't shake the feeling that I had failed them in some way. As

I walked to my car in the driveway, I mentally listed the things I had done right.

I rarely drink, I considered, hammering out the finer points of this argument while tossing yesterday's uniform to the back seat. *Promiscuousness is also not my game,* I thought as I shoved the car into reverse, rolling backward and tapping the return call button on the screen simultaneously. Heather picked up on the first ring.

"Let me guess, you're doing that JFK turn."

I groaned, not at all surprised that she knew. "Did they call you too?"

"They did, but I didn't answer."

"Me neither, at first."

"I can volunteer to take it if that helps?"

Heather's offer warmed me as she put aside her typical inflexibility. "Thanks, but no. I need to stay busy today."

"I take it the doctor's visit didn't go well?"

My heart sank. Words like *stage four* and *three to six months* flashed in my mind.

"She's dying, Heather." My throat bobbed. "My mother is dying."

Silence. Only a deep sigh could be heard as disbelief stole my friend's voice.

"I'm so sorry."

I made it a block out of the neighborhood when I stopped at a traffic light and slumped over the steering wheel, tears streaming down my face. "I can't believe this is happening."

"I-I didn't mean to blurt that out." Heather's voice sounded distant, as if she had put the phone down and was now moving around the room. "I'll be at your house in ten minutes."

When she hung up, I sat there, numb and unaware of time or location. That was until a car behind me honked, and I looked up to see the light had turned green. Hitting the gas pedal to the floor, the tires squealed before rubber caught the pavement. I left that other driver in the dust, took two right turns onto my street, and coasted into my driveway.

Gazing out the car's front window, I admired the small brick home I'd bought only six months ago. The porch lights on my first big purchase were still on, competing with the rising sun, which cast a golden glow over a winterized lawn. The smell of damp dirt crept in through the vents to greet me.

Get out. Get moving, my mind said, but my body wouldn't budge. I just kept staring at the rainbow colors glistening inside the wintry sunrays, floating in the air like tiny diamonds. *Such effortless beauty*, I thought. I wondered how anything that perfect could happen on a day like today. Then Heather's red Mustang pulled in behind me, and I quickly wiped the tears from my face.

"Why are you sitting out here?" Heather asked while tapping my car's window with the back of a hand. "Come on, let's get you inside."

Like a child led by a caring adult, I did as she suggested. Opening the door, she took me by the arm and helped me up the three steps to my house. Heather moved by rote, lifting a dormant plant nearby to find where I'd placed the hide-a-key. When she opened the door, she gave me a gentle nudge inside.

"Go take a shower," Heather said, taking my purse and the dirty uniform still in my hands. "And while you're doing that, I'll make you something to eat."

"Okay," was all I said before toddling down the hallway to do precisely as I was told.

Inside my bedroom sanctuary, I began to undress. Flipping the shower handle to hot, I pinned up my hair and stepped under the warm water, letting the jets rush over my shoulders and down my back. In the near distance, outside my room, I heard Elvis's voice flooding my home. A half smile twitched my lips.

For a moment, my heart warmed over Heather's thoughtfulness; she, no doubt, was trying her best to help. Then that good feeling plummeted over a realization that only a miracle could help me now.

As the steam from the shower filled my lungs, blurring the glass door so that the world outside felt unreachable, I wondered if I could hide here all day, all year. How long would it take before Heather came looking for me—an hour, maybe two? Would that be long enough for me to believe this was a bad dream? Like the shower door would open and magically the cool air would re-awaken me to discover that the last 12 hours had never occurred.

"Two eggs or one?" I heard Heather yell through the closed bathroom door.

My forehead rested against the cool bathroom tile, tears mixing with the water as I answered, "One's fine, thank you."

"You know," Heather began when I stepped into the kitchen, damp hair wrapped in a towel, "you really need better coffee!"

"What's wrong with my coffee?" I asked while twisting a hair towel into a high pile on my head before taking a seat on the benched side of the kitchen table.

"Medium roast?" She scrunched up her nose.

"It's just coffee."

Heather's mouth dropped open. "That's blasphemous!"

"Yeah. So, I'm a sinner," I muttered before taking my second much-needed cup of the day. She looked at me sideways as if trying to decide whether to ask but then said nothing.

Though Heather and I did not have the same religious upbringing, she believed in the negative effects of tempting spirits and the all-seeing eye of Mother Karma. Therefore, she would have found last night's ultimatum to God shocking, much like tempting fate. So, I thought twice before approaching the topic...

"Something out of this world is happening." I reached for the eggs, thoughts racing, as I struggled to decide what of yesterday to divulge and how.

"I'm sure that's how it feels." While Heather took the open bench next to me, I searched for the words that might help me to explain.

"No. I mean, seriously other-worldly."

Heather dropped her fork on the plate and looked up at me, eyes sparking with that look of curiosity I'd seen before. But it was her silence that urged me to continue.

"I saw something in the doctor's office yesterday." I turned away, unable to meet her wide gaze. "It was brief, just a flash of colors in my peripheral. Black and then white, but with an intensity I could feel. Like a premonition. Or an omen."

"An omen?" Heather repeated, pushing her plate clean away. "Sam, this isn't you."

Heather was that one friend, the kind every girl needs. The one with enough of an open mind that she can feel compassion for even the craziest of stories. And befriending a Baptist Preacher's kid like me, taught to fear anything unexplained by God, made this subject difficult if not taboo.

"I saw something. I just don't know what."

The room went still with my admission. Heather stared down at her hands, now folded on the table, contemplating her next words.

"You know I believe there's more to this world than we can see." She laid a hand on my shoulder. "And yesterday was stressful. But I wouldn't overthink it. Give yourself time to absorb all that happened."

She was right, of course, but fear drove me on. "What if what I saw was...death?"

"Girl! You've got to stop..."

With a sigh and a yank, the towel of hair was freed, wet hair falling over my shoulders. "I need to get on a plane and distract myself with the routine."

"I'm going with you." Heather made no eye contact as she chewed toast and sipped coffee.

"Excuse me?"

"I called Anna, the number one on your flight today, and asked if she wanted to drop her trip." She swallowed before continuing. "And she did. So, I took it."

My eyes began to fill for the uncountable time that day, and it was still early. Just yesterday, she'd finished a four-day trip and was now voluntarily going with me?

"Really?" My voice gurgled with emotion.

"Yes. Really." She finally looked at me, an easy smile widening over the coffee cup's rim. "But I swear, if the plane diverts to some dreadful city, I will blame you!"

And with that, we both laughed.

* * *

An hour later, I was clasping my lucky T.C.B necklace and adding the airline-issued scarf and blue vest to my attire when Heather walked out from the guestroom, fully dressed.

"I see you're 'taking care of business,'" she said, adding air quotes, a jab at my flying rituals and superstitions.

"I have a routine," I scoffed, running a lint roll down my skirt without looking up. "And no, I'm not changing it."

"Hey, how about we wear our uniform hats today?" Unexpectedly, she changed the subject, handing me the pill hat in her left hand. "I know it's neither 1960 nor popular, but they're regulation... Let's be different."

Without missing a beat, I reached for it. "What the hell?" I said before turning for the door, smirking as I grabbed my bag on the way.

"Well, what do you know, the preacher's kid curses."

We stepped out like royalty into a mid-morning sun, shielding our eyes. I dug for my sunglasses and car keys as Heather's two-inch heels clacked from behind. As we walked, our collective exhale turning to steam in the cold morning, I glanced over to see my neighbor, Mrs. Jefferson, collecting the morning paper. She was already waving.

"Good morning." I smiled a smile that didn't reach my eyes, absorbing the scene: Mrs. Jefferson, standing there in her red, silk pajamas with matching slippers, and us, looking like flight attendants from the movie *Catch Me If You Can* in our little pill hats, roller bags gliding behind us.

"Hello, Samantha dear!" Mrs. Jefferson spoke enthusiastically. "Where're you girls off to today? Las Vegas?"

Mrs. Jefferson had the impression that it was perpetually the year 1967 and girls in our position were always jetting off to Las Vegas, no doubt to see Frank Sinatra at The Sands Hotel.

"No, ma'am," I hollered, remembering her hearing loss. "It's New York City today!"

Her eyes grew wide. "Well, I'll be. Don't you girls live the life."

"Yes, ma'am," I said while unlocking my car. "We're truly blessed."

"You sure are, dear." She shook the rolled newspaper in our direction for emphasis. "Be safe now, ya hear?"

"Give my love to Mr. Jefferson," I said as she waved me off before stepping back into her home. "She'll live vicariously through us for the rest of the day," I muttered to Heather.

"Tell me again, why do we love our jobs?" Heather said, her tone biting as she settled into the passenger seat and tugged on the seat belt.

"It's not all that bad."

"Yeah, and maybe nobody will hand us their baby's crappy diapers today."

She had me there.

CHAPTER FIVE

(The Angel)

"For he commands his angels with regard to you,
to guard you wherever you go."

— Psalm 34:7

Angels like Gabriel and Michael respect the Old Testament scriptures, where battles between heavenly beings unfold. The God in the Hebrew Bible is powerful, quick to correct those who go astray, and quick to forgive those who repent. Every angel has faced moral choices, and Elvis was no different.

He'd carefully observed the strong angels who took on human forms for many years. They were given essential jobs of safeguarding and salvation. Many returned cracked and scorned, burdened by the weight of their trials. Yet Elvis longed for the challenge; he was resolved to validate his value—to show that he could elevate himself and accomplish his mission for himself and God.

After witnessing Samantha's incredible ability for second sight in the hospital, Elvis felt a sense of urgency. Although God had not yet called upon him or given clear guidance—something angels often experience—he was confident that his purpose was near. Over the last 12 hours, Elvis had come to understand how important Samantha was in the fight between good and evil. His role in her life was now more crucial than ever.

Seated at Gate 34 in Atlanta's bustling C concourse, Elvis leaned casually to the left, reading the morning newspaper beside an elderly man who reminded him of his gentle yet cautious father. The headlines warned of an impending housing market crash, leaving many concerned about how to protect themselves. He felt relief, grateful that worries about money and possessions were now behind him.

He heard Samantha's warm and familiar voice before he saw her. As he lifted his head, he saw her striding confidently toward him, a black, weathered travel bag rolling smoothly behind her. He smiled as he admired her professional outfit. It was well-fitted and looked polished, showing her determination.

"Hello, ladies," a gate agent wearing a red Santa hat approached Samantha and the friend he quickly recognized as Heather. "If you're ready, I'll let you down."

"Thank you," said his assigned beauty, keeping it brief but courteous.

"Could you give us a few minutes?" asked Heather. "We'd like to pray to the God of flight."

Elvis shook his head while they all laughed together.

"It's quiet on the front this morning," the agent said, opening the door to the bridge and stepping aside to allow Samantha and Heather to pass.

"Good. Then there's no need to spike everyone's coffee," Heather said as she entered first.

Heather was a girl after his own heart. He snickered, noting that while Sam merely shook her head at Heather's ever-cynical attitude, their fellow employee looked concerned.

"She's just joking!" Sam reassured her as she walked by, with Elvis trailing behind the two jostling women.

When he was a young man, Elvis had a fear of flying. His mother, Gladys, insisted that he travel by boat and train whenever possible. However, as his fame grew, he'd needed to travel farther and more quickly than ever, making air travel necessary. Before long, he purchased his first plane, and his love for flying began to develop.

As Samantha and Heather stowed their bags and engaged in small talk with other cabin crew members, Elvis settled into his seat in row two, fully aware that first class was Sam's designated work position. In his signature Elvis pose, he lounged in the window seat, his knees splayed wide apart, savoring the aroma of coffee wafting through the cabin. *Dear Lord. I miss coffee.* He closed his eyes to fully absorb the soothing scent.

It took only a few moments before the morning travelers began to board, each walking by Elvis one at a time. First-class passengers boarded the plane first, and he found himself intrigued by the diversity of the people. The first was a busy businessman in a tailored suit, his thoughts a mix of corporate strategy and family concerns. Next was a model headed to New York, her nervous energy palpable as she focused on her appearance. As the main cabin travelers boarded, he felt drawn to their simplicity and family-oriented nature.

"Good morning," Sam greeted a mother traveling with her son. "Welcome! I'm glad you're with us."

"I want to see! I want to see!" The young boy tugged on his mother's sleeve, pointing toward the cockpit. When Samantha saw his deep brown eyes excited over discovering something new, she immediately took action.

"What do you say? Shall we go ask the captain for a visit?" She crouched to his level, seemingly enjoying his eager bouncing while gently guiding him toward the cockpit. Inside, a man wearing a snowflake tie and a woman with reindeer ears were busy pushing buttons and adjusting headsets.

As he observed Samatha's interaction with the young boy, Elvis reflected on the changes in the world. A female pilot? That was certainly a new sight. He couldn't recall ever seeing a woman on a flight deck during all his flights with Samantha. It was a clear sign that times had changed since he last flew in the physical. *When was that? 25 years ago? No, far more.*

While reflecting on the past, Elvis noticed a stout man wearing a Stetson cowboy hat approaching him. The man stood at least six feet three inches tall, swaying slightly as beads of sweat trickled down from under his felt hat. Reflexively, Elvis stepped back, narrowly avoiding contact, as if a collision were possible. This reaction made him chuckle. Even if the man had brushed against his energy field, all Mr. Stetson would have felt would have been a rush of adrenaline, similar to the excitement or anxiety that the living often experience. However, Mr. Stetson showed no signs of hesitation.

Then, another man stepped up and came to a stop behind Stetson. The sun was barely seeping through the airplane's drawn window shades, yet this new stranger wore dark, reflective sunglasses as if he were already beachside in Hawaii. Elvis's eyes narrowed as he admired the stranger's hair.

I miss that jet-black look—mysterious yet still fashionable. He ran a hand through his naturally brown hair and wondered if The Boss would allow a change in hairstyle. He already knew the answer, but thinking about it made him laugh. In these lighthearted moments, Elvis rediscovered the joy of being invisible. It contrasted with when he stood on Sunset Boulevard, filled with worry as no one recognized him during a dare. *We've come a long way, baby,* he thought.

He was just about to wave Mr. Cool— as he decided to call him—onward, using the power of suggestion, when the stranger slid his glasses down his nose, looked him in the eye, and....winked!

"Well, I'll be a son-of-a—"

"Sir, are you alright?" When Sam's voice interrupted him, her concern pulled Elvis's attention away from Mr. Cool and back to the swaying Stetson hat man.

A rustle of concerned voices rose as Samantha raised a hand, halting the line of people behind her from boarding. The man in sunglasses was trying to support Mr. Stetson while Elvis mentally reached out to Mr. Cool, firing off a barrage of questions telepathically and insistently.

"Are you this man's guardian?" he screamed through the lines of consciousness that all angels share. "What's your name, friend?" But Mr. Cool's focus never wavered from his unsteady companion. Elvis muttered a curse under his breath.

"Can I get your friend some water?" Sam asked Mr. Cool, her blue eyes shifting towards Heather, who stood mid-plane helping two small children with their seat belts. Heather glanced up and slightly nodded as if she sensed Samantha's request.

"We're fine, miss. Thank you," Mr. Cool said as Mr. Stetson grumbled incoherently and slumped into a first-class seat by the window. Elvis winced when the man's head hit the wall with a thud.

Mr. Cool—whom Elvis considered an angel in the flesh—began to pull his friend upright by the shirt before finally taking the aisle seat beside him. As Mr. Cool fidgeted uncomfortably, as if trying to remove something he'd accidentally sat on, Elvis closed his eyes and projected his energy outward. Like a vivid line of blue runway lights, he traced it across the aisle until it settled over Mr. Stetson's faint aura, which glowed in a circle with broken links. He noticed Mr. Stetson's shallow breathing and sensed weakness, disorientation, and a pervasive ache from head to toe.

When Elvis opened his eyes, he said firmly through clenched lips, "You better start talking!"

"Is his friend okay?" Heather was suddenly at Sam's side like a united force. "Does he need medical attention?"

Elvis conveyed a silent plea for help, hoping that someone perceptive among the living would notice it. However, only Mr. Cool seemed to look his way. He observed the man's dark eyebrows furrowed as he peered at him over reflective sunglasses, glaring toward what was apparently the only empty seat in first class. Heather followed Mr. Cool's gaze, an awkward flush creeping into her cheeks.

"She's waiting," Elvis said with a smirk that curled his lip. To ensure the angel in the flesh understood, he pointed to Heather, who was now giving Mr. Cool a look that clearly indicated she was two seconds away from calling security.

"Thank you for asking, darling. Everything is just peachy." Mr. Cool turned his attention to Heather, speaking in a tone that conveyed Southern hospitality. "But if that water offer still stands, I'd love some."

With that, Heather turned and walked away, leaving Elvis to assume she would get the water. This left the two angels—one in the flesh and one in the spirit—to glare at each other. When another traveler stepped aboard, a woman wearing an Atlanta Braves ball cap, she passed between them, unaware of the heavenly conflict she had just entered.

"I know you can hear me, pal," he spoke calmly as Mr. Cool removed his dark sunglasses.

Shifting his position, he moved to see around the eager baseball fan and peered into the most profound, darkest set of eyes he'd ever seen on a man—whether human or angel. Mr. Cool's black pupils studied him as he folded the glasses in hands so large that he found himself praying he had not misunderstood the situation.

"What do you say we lay our cards on the table, friend?" Elvis suggested. "Seeing as we're serving the same God and all."

Or were they? He was starting to wonder.

Elvis didn't recognize the face that stared back at him, but that wasn't surprising; he had interacted with only a few angels over the years. In fact, he had only seen the messenger angel, Gabriel—the most active angel besides Michael—once, and that was from a distance. However, he knew that angels who take on human form present an impressive image. Whether it's a homeless man without legs begging for money on a street corner or the lumberjack of a man standing before him now, all creations evoke a sense of awe.

"Today shall be a test." When Mr. Cool finally spoke, his words were so soft; they floated like feathers carried by a wind. Elvis leaned forward, afraid they'd be lost to the next breeze if he wasn't careful.

"Who are we testing?" Elvis's attention was laser-focused, fearing he'd miss the big man's next word. He instinctively knew it would not be repeated.

"Not we, but I," the burly angel said, running a massive hand over his square jaw and stroking the five o'clock shadow already thick at ten in the morning. His coal-black eyes shifted to Samantha as he added, "Not you, but her."

Elvis stiffened. His attention shifted quickly to Sam, who was oblivious to the tense situation and offered coffee to the cockpit crew at the front of the plane. A sense of dread rose inside him as he turned back to see Mr. Cool reclining in his seat, his head tilted back and eyes closed. Beside him, Mr. Stetson leaned against the plane's window, starkly pale and motionless—his appearance contrasting sharply with his partner's relaxed demeanor.

"Start talking, Jack," Elvis said sharply, but Mr. Cool remained quiet.

CHAPTER SIX

(Samantha)

"Do not forget to show hospitality to strangers, for by so doing, some people have shown hospitality to angels without knowing it."

— HEBREWS 13:2

"You have a kook in row two," Heather spoke with a bored tone.

Standing near the cockpit, steaming coffees in hand, I gave her a withered look that said, 'You're acting wildly inappropriate...but I'm listening.'

"Must have been a full moon last night because his energy's...off." Heather shook her head while bending over to check the drink cart.

I moved in closer. "And by energy, you mean...?"

Although I had often heard suggestions that lunar cycles can influence human behavior, I also knew my friend. Heather's belief in spiritualism and everything supernatural indicated that we weren't just sitting around a campfire, stargazing and sharing scary stories. This was serious; every possibility was on the table. My friend's mind was a virtual grab bag of pixies and fairies. Coupled with my preacher's kid imagination, ghosts and demons were now in play, too, none of which thrilled me. If she'd truly meant all that went bump in the night, I would need more than just coffee to cope.

"His center of energy is clearly wobbly." Heather's eyes widened as if suggesting I should have known that before she moved on to the next worry. "And the man's friend is passed out at the window."

Finally, something I can understand, I thought.

Suppressing my frustration, I leaned out from the forward galley. Following Heather's logic, I peeked at the seat and sighed. I wasn't in the mood for this, but as cabin crew, our primary responsibility was to ensure the safety of our passengers.

"Alright." With a soft thud, I set the steaming brews to the galley ledge, taking a hands-on stance. "And how are these guys a problem, exactly?"

"The big fella wearing the too-cool-for-school shades..." She nodded in his direction. "He's been talking to someone in row two."

I peered over Heather's shoulder at the row in question. "There's nobody in row two."

"Exactly! We don't want an emergency at thirty thousand feet." Heather's eyes widened, and when I didn't move, she quickly nodded toward the cabin, adding, "We have to be sure all's good, right?"

"We should never have taken this trip." I faked a smile as yet another customer headed to their seat, hopeful sights set on New York City. "I just wanted a distraction and yet here we are."

"You know I've got a sixth sense when it comes to trouble," Heather said flatly.

How is this day even possible? I asked myself, hot coffee in hand and warming my fingers. As I looked over Heather's shoulder, the man in question relaxed in his seat, head tilted back, arms folded across his belly. His face looked peaceful. "I think he's sleeping." I moved deeper into the galley, out of sight. "Maybe we shouldn't bother him?"

"Something's off," said Heather with a sigh. "I can feel it—that man ain't right."

"Isn't," I retorted, to which Heather merely narrowed her gaze at me. "Okay, I'm going!"

Heather held back the boarding line while I approached the man in the aisle seat. The closer I got, the more I struggled with what to say, like, 'Excuse me, sir, but my friend thinks you are "off," can you explain that?'

Should I add the air quotes or not? I internally cringed as I stopped at the man's side, watching the gentle rise and fall of his chest. *He's breathing—that's a good start.*

"Excuse me, sir." I cleared my throat. "Would you or your friend like some coffee?"

The man jumped at my voice, his eyes flying open to look up at me. A smile spread across his unshaven face.

"No, ma'am," he replied, pushing a swatch of jet-black hair away from his eyes. "Joe and I are fine, but we thank you for the kind offer."

As he made that movement, a sweet scent of melons wafted through the air. The fruity aroma triggered a memory at the edge of my mind, just out of reach. The hairs on my arms stood up.

I shifted my focus to the man, Joe, slumped against the window. A sliver of sunlight peeked around the plane's drawn shade, casting a glow over his ashen face. I glanced back at Heather, who was still watching me from the plane's doorway. A line of passengers had deepened over her shoulder and her eyes widened with a question I didn't know how to answer.

"My apologies, sir, but..." I scrambled for the right words. "Is your friend feeling alright?"

The man's eyebrows rose in surprise, and he nudged his friend. "Wake up, Joe! The lady needs to speak with you."

Joe didn't move.

The next few seconds unfolded in slow motion. Joe's body slumped unnaturally forward, his cowboy hat tumbling over the seat in front of him, his chin falling to his chest while his hands went limp at his sides. Behind me, a woman screamed. The sound felt distant, and I don't remember reacting to it; my focus was solely on the burly man who began to slap Joe's pale face. That's when my training finally kicked in!

"Sir, is your friend diabetic?" The thought hit me like a lightning bolt. I turned to Heather, meeting her wide-eyed expression with an urgency of my own. "Get some orange juice."

Heather wasted no time, turning for the galley and passing the captain, who must have heard the commotion and stepped out of the cockpit.

"9-1-1." I pointed at him next. Then, glancing up the aisle of the plane, I witnessed our number three cabin crew member—no doubt regretting her day as well—as she moved travelers to the back of the plane. I couldn't hear every word, but her tone sounded firm and calm as she instructed the morning flyers to follow her toward the plane's back exit.

While my heartbeat pulsed in my ears, I turned back in time to witness the burly man pulling Joe upright, still trying to stir him. Nothing. No response came.

"Sir, please step away," I ordered as Heather arrived just in time with a small plastic cup of orange juice.

"You think he's diabetic?" she asked.

"It's a guess." I took the cup, adding, "I thought I detected a sweet scent from him earlier."

"Ketosis," Heather exclaimed and then ran off. I hoped she was headed for the galley and the other half gallon of orange juice chilling in the cooler.

When the captain shot a piercing glance at the boarding agent, his expression conveyed a clear message: passengers crowding the jet bridge should return to the waiting area. Curiosity sparked among the onlookers as they craned their necks to peer around the obstruction, drawn to the chaotic scene before them. I could hear their whispers of concern as a few customers nervously inquired about how long the delay would last and whether they would miss their connecting flights. I tried blocking the rising tension, focusing intently on the pressing situation.

"Sir, please step into the aisle," I ordered again. "Help is coming."

As the burly man released Joe, he said, "He was fine earlier."

A chill coursed through my body as I stood there, my breath hitching in my throat. My eyes locked on Joe, who slumped against the window in a grotesque portrayal of stillness. His head hung at an unnatural angle. The word *deceased* flickered through my mind, but I quickly pushed it away, unwilling to confront that horrifying possibility. I reminded myself that I had no real experience with death—not the kind that truly mattered. Anything to hold on to my composure. I couldn't afford to let my emotions spiral out of control; this was not the time for that.

"Damn it, Joe!" his friend cursed, drawing my attention back as he floundered in his seat, looking for what? I didn't know. I glanced around and noticed the cowboy hat lying upside down in the row ahead. As I leaned over to retrieve it, Heather arrived at my side with more orange juice.

"Can he drink it?" She was panting, no doubt from the same adrenaline I felt at that moment.

"No, ma'am," the man said. "He's unconscious."

Unconscious. The word erupted in my mind like a shock wave. Heather and I moved in unison, urging the man to step out of the row and into the open aisle. Once the seat was empty, we exchanged a glance. No words were necessary; we understood what needed to happen next.

"I'll do it," Heather quipped first, then slid into the open seat.

I watched my friend reach for Joe's wrist as she rested her body over the armrest. Memories of yesterday at the hospital flashed through my mind—the devastating news we had received there and the reality that, in an uncertain amount of time, my selfless mother might be gone.

No. I shook my head, trying to dispel the overwhelming visions flooding my thoughts. *I can't think about that now. Not today. Maybe never.*

"Any pulse?" I asked, nervously chewing on my thumbnail as Heather struggled with Joe's arm.

"I can't reach him. He's wedged!"

"Try the neck artery!"

"Copy that," Heather said as a draft blew against my back, and I turned in time to see four large men dressed in black jumpsuits storming the plane. They marched up the aisle, carrying what looked to be a heart monitor.

"Thank you, ladies," the more prominent man said. "We've got this."

Heather and I quickly stepped aside as the men moved around us. Joe's friend followed our lead, and we all stood in silence. While Heather carefully retrieved her abandoned cup of orange juice, which she had gingerly placed across the aisle as if a lifesaving device, I looked up and noticed our captain watching us from the airplane's forward doorway. I gave him a confident nod.

"Let's get him to a flat surface." When one of the medics spoke, my attention snapped back.

"On three," the other said, and a second later, the group lifted Joe up and over the seats until he lay flat in the aisle.

Two men went to work while the others quickly exited the plane. A younger-looking blonde gentleman wrapped a blood pressure cuff around Joe's arm while the older paramedic continued his evaluation, leaning closer to Joe's mouth and his now rapid breaths.

"Is your friend diabetic?" he suddenly snapped at Joe's friend, who merely shrugged in response.

"Blood pressure's elevated," the other young man stated. "Pupils fixed and dilated."

"We got to go." Still holding Joe's wrist, the leader looked towards the plane's front exit and screamed for a gurney.

Off in the distance, I heard..."Coming!"

My heart ached as I looked at Joe. His body lay so unnaturally still, a shocking reminder of the past 24 hours. A torrent of emotions surged within me, tightening around my chest, and tears spilled from my eyes, blurring my vision. I turned away, unable to bear the sight any longer.

As I lifted my gaze to the aircraft's ceiling, squinting against the haze, I struggled to make sense of what I saw: jagged, two-or-three-inch-long grooves etched across the interior like the claw marks of a colossal beast that had claimed the plane as its own personal scratching post.

"How in the world..." My words faded. I simply could not fret over one more thing.

As a single tear slipped from my eye, I felt an enveloping warmth surround me, like a soft blanket on a chilly night. It was a comfort that felt instinctive, drawing me in. "Easy now, honey," a gentle voice murmured in my ear like a soothing melody. "I've got you."

For a fleeting heartbeat, I envisioned these words as something internal, a primal survival instinct buried deep within me, striving to keep my senses anchored in the moment. But as that deep, resonant baritone drew closer, vibrating softly, the realization struck me—this was not my own voice.

The crash of a stretcher colliding with the plane's interior pulled me back to reality. In the periphery of my vision, a sliver of daylight sliced through the dimness at the aircraft's rear. Just a fleeting glance was all it took to divert my attention from Joe.

When I returned my gaze, the world around me had changed dramatically. The gentle, muted glow typically found in airplanes had vanished, replaced by a radiant beam of white light pouring into the first-class cabin. The brilliance enveloped me, overwhelming my senses and stinging my eyes like the sharp discomfort I felt as a child when I dared to stare directly at the sun. Instinctively, I lifted my hand to shield my eyes, attempting to block out the harsh illumination. Even with my vision partially obscured, I could see the paramedics working with urgency as they lifted Joe onto the gurney.

"The light!" The frantic tone of my voice was virtually unrecognizable.

Reaching out, I was grasping for someone, anything, and when I felt flesh and bone, I gripped it like it was the last lifeboat on a sinking ship.

"Heather?" I whimpered as my fingers encircled silky soft flesh, drawing the unknown closer as the sound of a stretcher rattled past, its wheels in dire need of oiling.

"Are you okay, Sam?" When Heather finally spoke, I reached in her direction, desperate for the comfort of a familiar touch.

"Heather!" The syllables in her name gurgled as my words were now laden with tears.

"You're shaking!" she exclaimed, and I held on tighter still. "Don't faint on me now. The medics are busy."

"The light, it's too bright…" I squeezed my eyes tighter.

"What light, Sam?"

It felt like I'd been dropped from one surreal dream into another stark reality. I blinked, and the soft, warm glow of the plane's under-bin lighting enveloped me. The medics were gone. Joe and his imposing friend were nowhere to be seen. As beads of sweat mingled with the tears on my face, I turned my gaze to the remaining crew members. As they prepared to exit, the captain and first officer hastily gathered their bags, a sense of urgency in their movements.

"Did you see the light?" I asked Heather again, my voice trembling as I wiped my tear-soaked cheeks, desperately searching her expression for understanding.

"No, I didn't see anything, Sam." She looked at me tenderly before suggesting, "Let's get you home."

"But someone took my hand." I wanted clarification, but Heather was already gathering our belongings as I glanced around the now-empty plane. "What about the flight?"

"There'll be no flight today," she said matter-of-factly while turning to face me, now taking both shoulders in a firm, attention-grabbing grip.

"Will Joe be okay?"

Heather leaned in, forcing me to look her in the eye. "Let's go home."

CHAPTER SEVEN

(The Angel)

*"Are not all angels ministering spirits sent to serve
those who will inherit salvation?"*

— HEBREWS 1:14

Elvis paced restlessly in the narrow confines of row two, alternating between standing and sitting in a space that felt too small for his racing thoughts. With each passing moment, he cautiously stepped forward, sensing a rush of eagerness, only to pull back as if caught in an invisible tug-of-war. His mind raced with countless questions. Since arriving in Angelhood, opportunities to meet with The Boss have been few. Today's events seemed well-suited for a council meeting, yet their collective communication was unsettlingly silent.

As Mr. Cool remained tight-lipped, Elvis reluctantly found himself grappling with the realities of humanity—praying and waiting for God's guidance. He'd become familiar with heaven's inner workings and developed an abundance of patience, a quality he had lacked during his life. Everything changed yesterday when Elvis observed Samantha's unexpected reaction to the demons at the hospital, drawn there by the family's grief. Now, Joe's soul was passing through the border light, heading toward Heaven or Hell; he wasn't sure which—and Sam was witnessing it all.

Samantha stood before him, her heart racing and her mind in chaos. The sight sparked a strong protective feeling in Elvis. As her fear grew, so did his wrath, his eyes burning with a rage reminiscent of the archangel Michael. Samantha was all he could see and care about at that moment. He instantly reached for her, pulled her close, and held her tight.

If what happened at the hospital brought them to this point, then Hell-be-damned, someone needed to inform him quickly. He was sure that both the living and the dead had learned over time that squandering was not a choice when confronting the devil. If the demons disclosed their plans, something significant was underway.

As Joe's soul rose into the border light, Samantha shook in his embrace, her blue eyes wide with fear. The crossing of souls, a profound and significant event, is comforting for angels, but the light feels akin to staring directly into the sun to the living who witness it. He quickly acted when Samantha raised her hand to block the bright light.

His wings spread wide, expanding outward like a guardian's shield. A moment later, he heard a ripping and grinding sound as the mighty, otherworldly wings carved deep grooves into the aluminum ceiling of the plane. The noise—a chilling echo of nails scraping against a chalkboard—sent shivers down his spine. He looked up and smirked because let's face it...wings were cool.

Standing firmly behind Samantha, he felt her inch closer, slipping beneath his wingspan and instinctively seeking safety. Although she was unaware of the power she held, her fingers gripped the first and second joints of his wings, sending a sharp pain shooting through his back. He sucked in a breath, clenched his teeth, and dared not move.

She didn't realize what she was holding while he contemplated the irony of the situation. A human man could be immobilized with a single grip, yet angels also had their vulnerable points. Unlike humans, however, it would take a formidable opponent to come as close as this beautiful woman was to him. Still, he refused to let himself be distracted by that—at least, not now.

The crossing light lasts only a moment—just a few seconds. That's when a soul must cast off earthly ties and return home. He braced himself for the resonating impact that all angels feel when two worlds collide. The spirit world and the mortal realm mixed like oil and water; one carried the weight of everything, while the other was merely a blemish on an otherwise perfect creation.

"Easy now, honey," he whispered in Sam's ear, gently taking her hand, which felt delicate compared to his own. "You're okay. I've got you."

"The light is too bright," Sam murmured as she shifted closer, pinning him against the plane's hull.

The tab on the window shade pressed uncomfortably against the back of his compromised wing. Although the discomfort was unpleasant, he chose to focus on the pain. The throbbing and tingling sensations racing through him created a strange feeling—an odd mix of pleasure and discomfort that only heightened his awareness of the physical world.

In his spirit form, experiencing physical touch from the living was a rare and cherished occurrence, a longing he rarely allowed himself to acknowledge. He understood how unusual that might sound—angels weren't supposed to crave intimacy; that was a human need. Perhaps his longing stemmed from the fact that he had been so deeply loved. He considered the possibility that his experiences differed from most angels. While that could be true, he would likely never know for sure. He couldn't simply ask anyone; he had never encountered another angel like himself.

"Heather?" she whimpered, her words choked with tears and overwhelming emotion.

"Are you okay, Sam?" When her friend finally arrived, Samantha grabbed her tightly and held on. "You're shaking!"

"Did you see the light?" Sam's voice raced with urgency, desperate to confirm whether her friend had seen the light, too. A glance at Heather's confused expression assured Elvis she had not.

Over the years, he'd watched many souls pass through the brilliant lights at the borders of heaven. The dazzling beauty of that brilliance never failed to amaze and captivate him; it was a testament to the splendor of the divine. It was remarkable how few near-death survivors remembered the experience because once you see it, you cannot unsee it. The light that beckons pales compared to the beauty of heaven—or the terror of Hell, for that matter. Though he had never seen Hell himself, he had heard the rumors.

Samantha whimpered as she finally loosened her tight grip on his wing and moved both hands to cover her face. His wing flexed back into place once her hold relaxed, and Elvis let out a relieved sigh. "Lord, have mercy," he muttered to himself.

Since Heather, the one person he had feared might someday catch a glimpse of his angelic glow, seemed unaware, he took a much-needed seat.

"No, I didn't see anything, Sam," Heather said, scanning her friend with a hurried yet thorough assessment. Seemingly satisfied, she tossed one last order over her shoulder as she reached for their crew bags. "Let's get you home."

Elvis found Heather's response curious as if nothing that had happened today had surprised her. *How often did this occur? Or was this some weird Heather thing?* The woman was as solid as iron, a mix of sugar, spice, and everything nice. While others tip-toed around Heather, he was convinced that even nature kept a watchful eye on this remarkable woman.

"Will Joe be okay?" Sam asked, gripping her friend's arm as she hurried to leave.

Heather lowered her gaze, studying the floor beneath her feet as if the right words were woven into the worn carpet. Pain and conflict flickered across her face. Her usual porcelain complexion was now red and blotchy, and her lips trembled. Then she shook her head as if to say *no*.

Heather leaned in, forcing Samantha to meet her gaze and said, "Let's go home."

Meanwhile, Sam just stared straight ahead. She delicately brushed a strand of hair away from her wet cheek, then turned and made her way to the front exit of the plane. Elvis observed as Heather followed her, grappling with Samantha and her luggage.

He walked just a few paces behind, admiring how Heather paused whenever Samantha stumbled. He noted the way Heather extended a hand in support and how Samantha eagerly and gratefully accepted it. The love he witnessed in that moment felt like a powerful life force. When the front door swung open to the C concourse, it was Heather who stepped through first.

The bright lights of Atlanta's airport came into view, accompanied by children screaming and dogs barking. Both women paused, taking in the bustling world around them. People chatted loudly over Bluetooth devices, seemingly engaging in meaningful conversations, as if speaking in person.

Finally, Heather sighed and said, "Well, if this isn't the crappiest morning ever, I'd be as surprised as Captain Jackson at a menopause seminar."

Elvis chuckled.

As they walked through the concourse, he could sense that Samantha was struggling with what she had witnessed. However, he understood that the real mystery was the enigmatic Mr. Cool. He had never encountered this figure before and wondered if he might be a high-ranking angel like Gabriel or Michael, which would explain why they had never interacted until now.

With that realization, he extended his senses outward, trying to focus on the otherworldly vibrations—the in-between doorway through which angels come and go, flowing like a river of good and evil through every aspect of life. Yet, he felt nothing. All was silent on the wayward front.

Although conducting a frequency test was standard practice to assess the safety and security of their charges, he had never viewed Samantha simply as an asset or an assignment. Ultimately, she was his responsibility, and their shared connection made her emotions easily detectable to the nearby angels. This made Mr. Cool's presence—a larger-than-life figure seemingly supervising Joe's ascension to the light—challenging to interpret.

Was it just a coincidence that Mr. Cool was there for Samantha that morning? He recalled the spoken riddle concerning a test. If this was indeed a test, did Sam pass? Deep down, he felt that they had, in fact, both failed.

* * *

The sun sparkled like diamonds on the wet airport parking lot. While snowfall during Christmas in Georgia is a rarity, the promise of rain is always looming. As he trailed behind Samantha and Heather, he intentionally stepped into the puddles, marveling at how the water danced beneath his soundless white boots. Each splash was exhilarating, yet somehow, his matching slacks remained untouched. Like a child discovering something new, he glanced up at the women ahead of him, his smile fading when he saw them walking silently with blank faces.

The living miss the miracles, he thought solemnly, reminding himself that he had missed many while alive. Despite his mistakes, he had done many things right, such as those cherished Christmas mornings spent with his daughter. He always made it a point not to work during Christmas; it was a special time for them. They would wake up early—well, early for his usual lifestyle—and if it snowed, they would rush outside to build snowmen in the front yard.

He felt happiest when his beloved Memphis experienced snowfall, even though it was rarely significant. If his memory was correct, the city had only seen a few substantial snow days— the kind that can bring the city to a standstill during Christmas—in 1939, 1948, and the one he remembered most vividly: 1975.

Life, he reflected, has a profound rhythm. Every moment serves a purpose—there is a time to cry, a time to laugh, and a time to confront the inevitability of death. God organizes our lives, yet people often take this blessing for granted, assuming that the sun will rise every morning. However, the ongoing battle between good and evil in the spiritual realm generates constant chaos. The nature of threats is ever-changing, keeping everyone on high alert.

With only two days left until Christmas, he sensed a change was imminent. The stars seemed out of alignment, and he wondered when someone—whether God or an angel—would reveal the details.

"Any time now would be great!" he hissed.

Following the two weary women, Elvis stayed close, determined not to let either of them out of his sight. As the ladies dragged their bags, the wheels sprayed a thin stream of water like a jet ski's wake. He kept an eye on the dark corners and empty stairwells. If things had gone differently, he would have slipped through time and space back to Samantha's house, where he could have relaxed and turned on the stereo for a quiet night. However, his every instinct warned him that peaceful nights were a thing of the past; the winds of change were stirring.

As Heather drove, Samantha sat in the front seat while he sat in the back. They were only a few turns into the drive when he realized they weren't headed to Samantha's house but Mr. and Mrs. Bennett's place.

"Are we going to tell your parents about what happened today?" Heather asked.

Samantha looked at her friend, her blue eyes glistening with emotion. Elvis resisted the urge to reach out and smooth the worry lines creasing her brow.

"No, I don't want to upset my family," Sam said, and Heather nodded in understanding.

As they turned down the last street in a middle-class neighborhood, where each house was beautifully decorated for the season, Heather relaxed her white-knuckled grip on the steering wheel. Elvis watched Samantha leaning casually against the interior door frame as the festive neighborhood passed by the window. He counted ten homes adorned with golden lights, each followed by another. He also noted the yard decorations: five Baby Jesus figures, six Santas, and ten reindeer, all adding a special touch to the scenery.

When Samantha spotted the three-bedroom, single-story brick home from her childhood, she sat straight in her seat. However, the question she asked next had nothing to do with her family or the house. "Were you holding me on the plane after they took Joe?" she asked, turning to her friend.

Elvis held his breath but remembered that angels don't need to breathe.

Heather continued driving, smoothly guiding Samantha's BMW into the Bennett's driveway. She shifted the car to park and turned off the engine. To ease her stress—or perhaps to help herself remember—she rubbed a finger across her forehead once, then twice. In fact, Heather massaged her temples so many times that Elvis imagined a genie might pop out of her ears to grant her a wish.

"As far as I know, I didn't touch you," Heather finally said, leaning closer to Sam.

"Are you saying you didn't whisper 'take it easy' in my ear?"

Elvis pressed his forehead against the back of Samantha's headrest, his thoughts racing with the realization that Samantha had heard him. Somehow, his words of comfort had slipped through the veil, crossing from the spirit world to the physical realm—but how? How was this even possible, and why?

"Sam—" Heather began, but Samantha wasn't listening.

"I felt arms around me," Samantha said, wrapping her arms around herself as if to demonstrate. "It was real!"

Heather took her friend's hands in hers. "Sam, I believe in miracles, ghosts, and everything in between, but...you're under too much stress."

Samantha sighed heavily, turning to gaze out of the car's front windshield. The door to the modest home creaked open, and Elvis tilted his head slightly.

"You need rest," Heather continued, noting that Sam's attention had shifted to the home's front porch. "You should spend time with your family."

Heather glanced in the same direction, squinting her eyes at Mrs. Bennett standing on the porch in a cozy, pink housecoat. Mrs. Bennett was waving as Samantha flung open the car door and stepped out into the cold.

"That was a fast flight, ladies!" She smiled brightly, like a child on Christmas morning.

CHAPTER EIGHT

(Samantha)

"For it is written: 'He will command his angels concerning you, and they will lift you up in their hands, so that you will not strike your foot against a stone."
— MATTHEW 4:6-11

She looked unwell; that was my first thought. As we pulled up to my parents' home, I saw my mother for the first time since the previous evening. Her smile was warm, but I noticed the familiar concern on her face—something I had seen countless times before. I told myself it was just my imagination running wild as Heather parked the car. But after everything

I had experienced that morning, I knew anything was possible.

As I opened the car door and stepped out, I tried to avoid noticing the changes in her appearance: her creamy complexion seemed paler, and her green eyes appeared sunken and dull. Instead, I forced a smile, though seeing my conservative mother standing on a cold porch in a robe, facing both God and the world, made my heart ache a little more. Despite her battle, cancer had not taken away her smile; it was still significant, just as I remembered it. It was the smile of a warrior—a symbol of her resilience that I prayed never to forget.

"Hurry, girls! It's cold!" Mother waved, calling out as if we had just exited the school bus.

The scene looked like something straight out of a Christmas movie. I had to admit that I didn't deserve to call this beautiful woman "Mother." She was as pure as the driven snow. While Daddy and I were far more humanly flawed than she was, it seemed clear that God knew what we needed, and that couldn't have changed, could it? Indeed, He wouldn't—couldn't—take her from us now.

The day's emotions mingled with the cold, which caused even more tears as Mother stomped her feet on the patio, urging us to hurry. From the other side of the car, I heard Heather laugh out loud.

"Sam, take your mother inside before she gets sick! I'll get our bags!" she shouted against the wind.

Before she gets sick? That phrase puzzled me. Could anything be worse than cancer? I found it ironic to worry about a cold when death felt so imminent. I hurried up the four porch steps two at a time, grunting as I passed beneath the colorful *Happy Birthday Jesus* banner that had replaced the American flag for the season. As the banner fluttered gently in the crisp winter air, I remembered how my father playfully referred to all the Christmas yard signs as birthday party decorations, turning the festive season into a whimsical celebration in our home.

"You should go inside, Momma," I said as I stood beside her, hugging and kissing her cheek.

"How was your flight?" she asked.

"We never left." I tried to sound casual as I held the door for Mother, and when I saw Heather approaching, I held the door for her, too.

"The flight was canceled," Heather added, leaving our bags inside the doorway before moving deeper into the house. "A man became...ill."

"Oh no," Mother said, as she turned towards the kitchen, heading for what I guessed was her beverage of choice: hot tea. "What's the poor man's name?"

"Joe," Heather and I replied in unison, then exchanged glances, silently warning each other to avoid any details.

Mother stood at the stainless-steel sink, her hands skillfully maneuvering the teapot beneath the steady flow of cool water. The soft sound of the faucet created a serene backdrop while her gaze remained fixed on her task. I noticed the intensity in her eyes; she was committing that name to memory like a dedicated stone mason. She then carefully measured the loose-leaf tea, always a process she performed with precision and care, before pouring hot water into the teapot. I understood that she was preparing for the quiet moments that would follow later—when she would kneel by her bedside and offer heartfelt prayers to the Lord on Joe's behalf.

"We should pray for Joe."

My stomach flipped when Mother spoke the words I had sensed on her face. I thought about what she didn't know: Joe could be standing at heaven's gate right now, and his family might be unaware of his fate. A lost loved one at Christmas time, I reflected. Suddenly, the tea didn't sound so appealing.

"We'll be praying," I agreed, surprising myself by including Heather in the task. I noticed her eyes widen in reaction.

"That's good, honey," Mother said, gesturing toward the kitchen table and inviting us to sit.

"Is Daddy here?"

"Your daddy's at the church."

A few moments later, the tea began to whistle from the stove, and the room fell silent as each of us seemed lost in our own thoughts. Heather and I watched as Mother poured hot water into an antique teapot, filling it with her chosen loose-leaf tea. I guessed it to be black English tea, as she usually preferred English varieties best, though Irish flavors often came in a close second.

"I bet you'd like to spike that tea right about now," I teased in a low voice. Heather pursed her lips, considering the idea while I grinned in a friendly challenge.

"About as much as you want fresh-baked brownies," she laughed.

Dang, she was right. I did want freshly baked goods, but not just any sweets—what I craved was the kind that someone puts effort and pride into, straight from the oven. Baking was my therapy, but since I wasn't in my kitchen, I would have to find another source of comfort. I glanced over Heather's shoulder toward the living room, contemplating my next move.

"Did Daddy get a new needle for the turntable?" I didn't wait for Momma to answer. I headed straight for the 1975 oversized floor console to see for myself.

The furniture from my childhood was enormous and made of solid oak. Its top, when opened, was so heavy that I needed help lifting it as a child. My father didn't mind this; he preferred that I stay away from his prized possession. I became so fascinated with his antique music machine that my dad eventually bought me a refurbished version. That record player still sits on a dresser in my childhood bedroom down the hall.

"You can't beat the vinyl crackle," my daddy would say. And, of course, he was right.

"Put something nice on, Sam dear," I heard Momma say. When I glanced back, I saw her sitting at the kitchen table, pouring Heather a cup of tea. "Play something that complements our beverages."

The sight warmed me; having tea with my mother was always special. Even as a child, I enjoyed many tea parties with real tea—not pretend. However, as I matured, Mother struggled to understand my generation's fascination with coffee. The rich, roasted aroma of freshly brewed coffee was an experience in itself, something I'd order effortlessly through mobile apps—a concept as foreign to her as the idea of intergalactic travel. In her eyes, it lacked the warmth and romance she associated with our cherished tea traditions.

My fingers danced across the textured surfaces of Daddy's album collection, tracing the spines of records that held decades of music history. Each hard edge I flipped revealed Gospel legends like CeCe Winans, Bill & Gloria Gaither, and The Jordanaires, with each voice echoing a different time and emotion. Yet, in this moment of reflection and need, my heart longed for one distinct sound. When I glimpsed the iconic visage of Elvis Presley, my hand halted, mesmerized by the magnetic charm radiating from his photo.

The 1971 album "You'll Never Walk Alone" resonated with me. The stage lights illuminated a photo of Elvis wearing a white jumpsuit with long fringed sleeves flowing down each arm. The crisscross laces of his suit were provocatively open at the chest, highlighting his handsomeness. Just seeing that face relaxed my soul. Although this was a Gospel album, it could have easily belonged to a mainstream genre, showcasing Elvis's crossover genius.

With a flick of the switch, the oak console hummed to life. It spun slowly and methodically, its rhythm comforting. Careful not to bend the worn edges, I removed the cardboard cover from the stack. The sleeve slid out as I turned it upside down, and the black vinyl dropped into my palm. Avoiding the grooves, I spun the record, balancing it between my palms, and blew gently, sending dust particles floating within the sunbeams.

When I placed the record on the turntable and lowered the needle, Elvis Presley's rich baritone filled the room, warm and inviting like a crackling fire in winter. "When you walk through a storm," he sang, and I exhaled my first full breath.

"Will you be assigned another flight?" Mother asked as she slid a teacup over to me. I took a seat.

Heather spoke first, "They gave us a few days off."

My mother's eyes widened, her gaze shifting to me as if she were waiting for clarification. I swallowed nervously, aware that Elvis was still singing from the living room.

"It...it's normal after an incident." I looked down at the steaming tea in my hands, as if the answers lay within the creamy brew. "They'll want a written report."

My mother might not have known much about the airline business, but she understood enough; if written documentation was needed, it meant something bad had happened.

"That poor man," she sighed, reaching across the table to place a hand on mine.

A collective sigh echoed through the room as we all absorbed the weight of the day. I shifted my gaze from the tea long enough to glance at Heather, whose eyes glistened with high emotions.

"He didn't look good, Momma," my voice cracked.

"I'm sure you girls did your best," she said, offering her free hand to Heather.

Did we truly help? I wanted to believe we did, but I had to accept the outcome. Joe's time on Earth had ended. I reminded myself that there was no way I could have known Joe's condition. He had walked past me, yes, but I barely spared him a second look; I was too distracted by my own grief. I would have to live with that realization and the questions that now haunted me.

"Heather did an excellent job," I sniffled. "She tried to help while I...well, I froze, Momma."

There was no simple way to articulate the blinding light that engulfed me, leaving me dazed and disoriented. It shimmered with an otherworldly brilliance, a dazzling spectacle that felt strange yet oddly welcoming. The light seemed to possess a life of its own, bending the very fabric of reality around it, as if it held the power to reshape existence at will. I could feel its energy surging through me, a warm current pulsing in sync with my heartbeat, radiating a soothing glow that spread through my bones, enveloping me in a cocoon of comfort.

"She stayed by his side," Heather said urgently, her voice trembling as she turned toward Mrs. Bennett. "He was a large man, ma'am. Sam couldn't have moved him. None of us could."

As the horror of that devastating moment came crashing back, tears streamed down my cheeks, free-flowing and unrestrained. "I...I had the bottle of orange juice in my hand."

My mother's eyes widened, confusion clouding her features as her brows knitted together. The cups of tea on the table were left to cool, while in the background, Elvis crooned softly about an existential question: "Who Am I?"

"I didn't realize." I swiped at the tears streaking down my face, clinging to the only truth I was sure of. "Maybe if I had noticed him sooner..."

I hesitated; my voice caught in my throat. If God was listening—and an instinctive feeling told me He was—He already knew of my profound disappointment in both Him and myself. Like a flickering candle, a small flame of anger began to smolder within me when suddenly, Heather's watch chimed, slicing through the heavy silence.

We exchanged worried glances, dread weighing heavily in our hearts. I watched in muted anxiety as my friend turned her wrist and read the message glowing on the screen. When she looked up at me, I sensed the finality in her expression. My stomach twisted, and I tilted my head in a silent plea, but she shook her head slowly, confirming what we had only heard whispered amidst the chaos: Joe had indeed passed.

Through the kitchen's expansive bay window, I gazed out at the delicate snowflakes drifting silently from a grey winter sky. Snowfall was an unusual sight in Atlanta, each flake gliding gracefully to the ground, light as a feather, swirling mid-air like tiny dancers caught in a gentle breeze.

I followed their serene descent as they landed softly on the brick windowsill outside, only to disappear, vanishing as quickly as they had come. Their fleeting beauty reminded me of my introduction to Joe—so vividly present one moment and then suddenly gone the next. Tears swelled and rolled down my cheeks, and I surrendered to them, allowing the grief to wash over me.

I felt my mother's comforting arms wrap around me, squeezing me tightly as she murmured soft reassurances—"Come here, baby girl," and "You'll be okay."

Heather and I were in no condition to drive home, so when my mother suggested we stay over for the night, we eagerly accepted. It brought back memories of childhood sleepovers, and I offered to share my cozy room and a comfy pair of pajamas with my friend. Although we might have been too old for sleepovers at our parents' places, Mother firmly decided we weren't going anywhere tonight. Thankfully, Heather seemed just as pleased with the arrangement.

PATRICIA GARBER

"Your father will be home shortly," she announced with a warm smile as she prepared fresh sheets and blankets for the bed.

Seeing her bustling around the room instilled a feeling of comfort and safety within me. I watched as she carefully folded the linens, her movements graceful and efficient, radiating a maternal warmth that made the house feel even more inviting. As she dropped the final sheet onto the mattress, a wave of affection washed over me at the sight of momma sinking back into her usual role—the forever-doting wife and mother.

When she leaned over to plant a soft kiss on my cheek, she paused for a moment, her gaze lingering on my face. Her eyes sparkled with contentment, and with a playful wink, she turned to leave, gently closing the door behind her, leaving the room enveloped in cozy stillness.

"Who was the last person to sleep in this bed?" Heather asked, eyeing the queen-size mattress as if she didn't sleep in random hotels 16 nights a month.

I laughed openly. "Aunt Mildred, last Fourth of July."

A slow smile spread across Heather's face as she sat at the end of the bed and bounced it. "Right side or left?"

"Left."

When I sat next to my friend, her eyes flickered around the room, and I could see Elvis's baby blues staring back at us from the posters still hanging on every wall.

"Good Lord, you took your Elvis seriously," she remarked.

We both erupted into laughter.

"I do take him seriously." I nudged her playfully with my elbow.

Heather fell backward, lying flat on the bed, her eyes fixed on the ceiling. Following her lead, I relaxed, expelling a long breath while admiring the poster pinned there for the better part of 10 years. That lopsided grin and mischievous sparkle in the blue eyes of the King of Rock and Roll made me smile.

"I especially love this one," I sighed dramatically.

"I bet you did!" Heather clicked her tongue and quickly corrected herself. "I mean, I bet you do. Love it, that is."

Now she gets it, I thought, stretching out each limb and relishing the sensation of every muscle easing for what felt like the first time that day. Deeper in the house, Elvis's voice—the backdrop to the day—had gone silent. The record must have played out, I thought. Mother, no doubt immersed in her cooking mode, hadn't noticed.

"What was on your childhood wall?" I asked, knowing that this topic would be far less complicated than the one that still haunted the day.

"Old movies, mostly." Heather's gaze drifted away as if she were being transported to some moment from her far-off childhood. "Cary Grant, Audrey Hepburn, and... oh, and Paris!"

"That makes sense," I replied.

* * *

The afternoon slowly drifted away from the sad memories that haunted us. When Daddy arrived home, the four of us gathered around the table, thanked God, and shared a meal prepared with loving hands. Those same hands that had comforted Heather and me just hours earlier now nourished our bodies as much as they had soothed our souls. We enjoyed fried chicken, collard greens, and banana pudding for dessert until our bellies felt ready to burst. No one mentioned Joe. Reliving the morning's events would have required too many questions for my father's sake. Daddy would press for details I still didn't have answers to, so it remained unspoken for the rest of the night.

"By the way, Sam, I noticed the turntable was left on." I huffed, feeling ten years old again, and he looked at me sideways, shaking his head.

"I'm sorry."

Despite my father's playful demeanor, he looked tired, his eyes red and watery. I gathered it was from lack of sleep. But when our gazes met, the love of God and family still glimmered in his smile.

Why wasn't he angry? How could he preach words like mercy and healing when God hadn't given us any?

"What artist did you play?" This was always my daddy's next question, right after the reprimand about the dangers of leaving a needle on vinyl too long.

"Guess." I grinned, though the smile never quite reached my eyes.

CHAPTER NINE

(The Angel)

"Then I looked and heard the voices of many angels, numbering thousands upon thousands and ten thousand times ten thousand. They encircled the throne and the living creatures and the elders."
— REVELATIONS 5:11

The soft, soothing sound of women peacefully sleeping permeated the atmosphere in the dimly lit room. Elvis settled into a plush, velvety blue chair in the far corner, its rich fabric inviting him to stay. He rested his forehead on a single finger, posture relaxed yet contemplative, with one leg crossed over a knee and foot bouncing. His striking blue eyes, bright and sharp like sapphires, stayed firmly fixed on the scene unfolding around him.

What had he possibly missed today? The question spiraled in his mind like a restless whisper, a tantalizing mystery begging to be solved. A persistent worry indicated that there was something he had missed, something obvious, yet he couldn't fully understand it—at least not yet.

How does a preacher's daughter go from a shy, humble lady to witnessing the departure of souls? And what was Mr. Cool's part in all this? As time passed, he continued to analyze the mystery, each time coming up with more questions, like "If Mr. Cool was aware of what was going on, why didn't he provide an explanation?"

In a distant corner of the room, an ancient heater sputtered to life. He jumped slightly, a wave of apprehension coursing through him as his jaw clenched, the muscles flexing under the weight of his unease.

Outside, winter winds howled. Inside, the air was filled with an energy that hinted at the shadows lurking beyond, and he realized that surrendering to it would cause the room to pulse with an eerie vitality. The fragile barrier between realms might lift, as at the hospital, revealing an unsettling presence: demons with malicious intent, watchful angels, and wandering souls flickering like candle flames in the dark.

To quiet his racing thoughts, he began to hum, a habit that had served as his sanctuary for a long time. The melody flowed from him like a gentle stream, familiar yet elusive—one that tugged at the edges of his memory with nostalgia. Though he couldn't grasp its name, the song transported him to a simpler time, a cherished fragment of his childhood.

In his mind's eye, he found himself back in a quaint one-room shack in Tupelo, filled with the warmth of countless memories. As he drifted further, his eyes roamed Samantha's room, taking in the lively Elvis Aaron Presley memorabilia on the walls—each piece a glimpse into his lasting legacy, a vibrant nod to a time both distant and familiar.

He pursed his lips, trying to recall how long it had been since he last saw this room. How long since he'd confronted the merchandised representation of himself? He tried to remember the details of each photo. Was that one taken in 1960 or 1962? While the timeline of his life was evident, the specific dates and times were hazy in his memory.

Samantha shifted in her sleep, and his gaze was drawn to her in the stillness. Strands of brunette hair fell across her eyes, making her nose twitch as she tried to move them away. With a flick of his finger, he shifted the hairs back to their rightful place and chuckled, a tenderness evident in his eyes.

"Much better," he said with a smile, showing his usual lopsided grin. Then, he saw something move.

A silhouette winnowed into the room like a wisp of mist caught in a soft, playful breeze. Standing tall, Elvis adopted a wide fighting stance, his body taut and ready for any challenge. The visitor continued to shift and morph, their shape flowing and bending in a fluid dance that captivated his attention. Finally, with effortless confidence, Mr. Cool stepped fully into the room. He emanated a magnetic charm, the atmosphere shifting with his entrance as if the room acknowledged the arrival of someone genuinely remarkable.

Elvis groaned as he shook his head in disbelief. "I should beat the devil out of you," he said as Mr. Cool smiled a slow, unworried grin, then held up a finger to suggest he might want to rethink that. "Smart aleck."

Like a celestial spotlight, a white beam of light began to circle above. At first, the beam was a narrow, delicate thread, barely noticeable. However, with each passing second, it swelled and expanded, spinning and growing with every rotation. The anticipation of what might be revealed beyond this rare and wondrous light phenomenon hung heavily in the air.

As the circle grew more extensive, reaching an impressive diameter reminiscent of a car tire, it began to fracture open, and countless tiny particles cascaded downward, shimmering like specks of dust in starlight.

Elvis remained rooted, his gaze locked onto Mr. Cool, who seemed transfixed by the spectacle above. With his eyes closed, Mr. Cool embraced the now-dusty beam of light. This stream, a conduit of divine energy, was a rare and powerful sight.

"Great, just perfect," Elvis muttered in frustration, his magnificent wings stretching out for the second time that day as he glanced over at the bed of sleeping women.

Mr. Cool lifted his chin into the light, allowing it to envelop him. Like healing waters, the stream peeled back layer after layer to reveal another form. Though this transformation was shocking, just one look at the hulking figure morphing into a warrior—spear in his right hand and a mirror of jasper in the other—made it clear to Elvis who stood before him: Gabriel, God's Holy Messenger. The sudden appearance of this divine being made Elvis tuck his wings tightly at his side, a gesture of surprise and respect.

"Hail, full of grace, the Lord is with you!" Gabriel suddenly boomed through Elvis's consciousness, leveling a fiery gaze his way.

Elvis looked around, feeling confused. Perhaps it was nervousness; he wasn't sure. But honestly, he couldn't believe he was face-to-face with God's messenger angel, who was addressing him directly. As Gabriel's presence illuminated his thoughts, the puzzle pieces began to fall into place: Samantha, the hospital, the demons, and the plane. Each element started to align in his mind, providing a clearer understanding of the day's events.

When clarity struck him, Elvis's eyes widened as the white-robed messenger—reminiscent of the Biblical story of Moses and the burning bush—snapped his fingers, igniting an all-encompassing halo of light, and...vanished.

Elvis stood dumbfounded and engulfed in darkness—spiritual darkness. Unlike his angelic eyesight, which rivaled military-grade night vision, these eyes could not see his own hand in front of his face. His heart raced, pounding inside his chest against genuine flesh—he paused to consider that term. Slowly, ever so, he slid a now sweaty palm across his tight abdomen and felt his stomach muscles flinch.

"Hot damn!"

When he considered the expletive, he heard his voice in real time and quickly slammed a hand over his mouth. *They don't teach this in angel school.* He chuckled. Because angel school didn't exist. New angels didn't have orientation days or welcome-to-the-club parties. First, there was death, followed by years of denial and retraining—not much fun.

As his vision adjusted, he took slow, unsteady steps backward, fixating on the movement of his black boots from heel to toe. Hadn't he been wearing white earlier? As he thought about this, his shoulders collided with the far wall, causing him to wince as the impact reverberated down his back, registering pain in a deeply profound way.

He lifted a trembling hand to his eyes, tilting his head to get a better look. The slim, bent fingers looked vaguely familiar. Then he turned his hand palm up, and his attention fell on one pinky finger, crooked at the knuckle. A smile spread across his face.

"Now that's some kind of miracle." He exhaled a low chuckle. When he drew another ragged breath, one dark eyebrow lifted as cool air brushed past his lips. "Fantastic."

He shifted his weight, stretching one long leg outward into a relaxed stance, savoring the sensation of his solid, human body. For a brief moment, a worry crossed his mind, making him question whether this was just a dream. Could angels even sleep? He doubted it—he hadn't in years. Yet, he was still young, as angels go. So, with the same hand he had just been admiring, he slid his palm downward. His chest felt solid.

While he couldn't clearly see the specifics of his attire, he recognized that it was a deep, dark hue, possibly blue. The fabric felt exquisite against his fingers, soft and luxurious like silk. As he ran his hand upward, he slipped it gently through the shirt's open collar, feeling the warmth of the skin beneath his touch. A thrill surged through him as he grasped the reality of everything—he had skin!

"Get a hold of yourself, man," he commanded, closing his eyes to calm his rapid breathing. That was when he heard...her.

His eyes snapped up just in time to see Samantha sitting unsteadily on the edge of her bed. As his mind raced, he searched for a quick escape but found no back door, fire escape, or way out. He paused when he noticed her long, brunette hair, which was in disarray, reminding him of when she was six—sleepy and rubbing her eyes insistently until they were bloodshot. The memory calmed him.

He recognized this child, this woman. After all, she was his Samantha. Nothing had changed. Well, that wasn't entirely true, he thought. Something had changed; she was no longer a child but all grown up. His train of thought paused when his gaze locked onto the pink carpet beneath a shiny boot. A sense of familiarity fluttered just out of reach. Didn't he have pink carpet once? Probably. He'd always liked pink.

Elvis never heard her approaching.

Across the room, Samantha stood. As she wobbled towards him, her head down, his eyes slowly rolled up, reminiscent of a scene from a horror film. One step, and she'd stop. Two steps, and she'd stop. With each step she took, he retreated farther into the room. His heart raced uncontrollably, and he feared he might hyperventilate and pass right out.

In the brief moment before Samantha stopped directly before him, he felt a surge of determination. With his back against the wall, he turned his head, aware that his quickened breaths could potentially wake her. He could hear her muttering something that unmistakably sounded like his name, breathy and inviting, before she slapped a hand against his chest with a decisive thud.

"No, don't go," she giggled.

Don't move, was his first thought when Samantha laid her head on his chest. The smell of her lavender shampoo wafted up his nostrils, evoking an even deeper inhale. Lavender and something else... *Was it mint?*

He hadn't physically experienced a scent in so long that he impulsively leaned in closer. His chest expanded; the idea of simply inhaling fascinated and enthralled him. As he inhaled another deep breath, pulling in the lingering scent of Samantha's sweet femininity, a deep sensation began to awaken within him.

No, no, no! he silently screamed, determined to keep that long-ignored, very masculine side of himself from getting too close to her softness. It wasn't that he didn't desire or yearn for her; his body practically shouted for her. His palms felt damp, and his pulse skipped over the feel of her touch.

Just think. Think. Elvis refocused, glancing toward the exit on the right and the full-size poster of himself that hung there, dated 1962.

While Samantha continued her feminine assault, shifting her mouth closer to the nape of his neck, Elvis lifted his chin towards the ceiling, virtually running from her lips. When Samantha slid her hand down the front of his sleek shirt, her fingers slipped between the buttons to caress the soft, brown hairs across his chest. His entire body tensed.

Down boy, he coached his body as Samantha snuggled closer. He was calculating how and where to exit with his eyes lifted to heaven. His mind was reeling, his body heated and out of control. He wasn't even sure if he still had angelic powers. Maybe he was purely human? He was mentally scripting a complaint letter to The Almighty when Samantha suddenly grabbed his face with her two hands.

"Sleep tight, sweet Elvis," she said before yanking him closer, planting a soft and supple kiss on his lips. He melted into her mouth.

The sensation of her wet lips, the taste of sweet moisture mingling with her lip balm, melted his core. His mind drifted away. He'd missed this—the act of kissing.

When her tongue brushed against his own, he moaned loudly before wrapping his arms around her tiny waist. He was pulling her closer when, just as suddenly as it had begun, the kissing stopped.

He was licking at her taste when Samantha suddenly reached for the doorknob and—froze. He squeezed his eyes shut. *Oh God.* He gritted his teeth. His mind raced, rewinding to Gabriel and how he'd watched as he snapped this gift of flesh into place.

Could it be that easy? Closing his eyes, he sent up one more plea. "Now would be a good time, Lord!"

And with a snap of his fingers—he was gone.

CHAPTER TEN

(Samantha)

"Then I saw another angel flying in midair, and he had the eternal gospel to proclaim to those who live on the earth—to every nation, tribe, language and people."

— REVELATION 14:6

Dear Mother,

You died on a Tuesday. As your soul left this earth, we watched the light fade from your eyes. I kissed you goodbye while the heart inside me died. My anger was stacked, brick by brick, around the grief like a fortress of solitude. With whom will I now share the exciting news about my wedding and my first child? With whom will we celebrate birthdays, anniversaries, and holidays? They're just days now, dates on a forever-empty calendar.

I'm a woman left without the one person meant to guide me through the challenges of womanhood. There are no more kitchen conversations about life and love; every word spoken is now a one-sided graveside chat.

Anger is consuming my spirit, overshadowing my upbringing—and I'm letting it happen. Daddy tries to help, but I don't need church right now; I need to be mad. He doesn't seem to understand my disappointment, disgust, and the rejection I feel towards a God who allowed this to happen. While I love Daddy, I'm taking a break from him. He still calls constantly and tries to connect. But the best I can manage is a text reminding him, "I love you."

I have no voice except when I say, "I love you, Momma. I miss you. I wish you were here."

Forever—Your Baby Girl.

"You have such a pretty view," I murmured, my tone laced with sorrow and yearning, as I took in the serene beauty of the cemetery. Sitting cross-legged on a patchwork blanket lovingly made by the ladies from the church, I carefully arranged fresh red roses, setting aside the wilted buds to dry. Beside me stood a granite stone etched with the flowers she cherished most—a beautiful blend of roses and daylilies. A cross adorned her marker, and I couldn't help but think how much she would have appreciated that symbol of faith. Although it held great significance, I found it hard to fully acknowledge; my gaze remained fixed on my mother's name: Evelyn Lynn Bennett, wife, mother, and faithful servant.

Daddy once told me, "It's okay to be angry with God; He understands our nature. Remember, the devil will use that anger for his own purposes." I believed him then, and I hold onto that belief still. Yet, deep down, I can't shake the feeling of indifference within me. My faith, once a source of comfort, now feels like a battleground of doubt and anger.

While collecting the dried flowers and putting them into a mason jar for future use, I took a moment to hear the rustling leaves around me, moved by a soft spring wind. The Oakland Cemetery was peaceful and nearly empty. I assumed the slow ambiance was due to the day of the week; perhaps people were too caught up with the hustle and bustle of life rather than reflecting on death on a Tuesday. I didn't mind, though; I appreciated the solitude. The time spent alone with my mother was precious. I shut my eyes and reclined on the blanket beneath me, concentrating on the distant sounds of the busy city a few blocks away in downtown Atlanta.

When I opened my eyes again, I saw colorful pink and white flowers above me. The grand magnolia tree swayed gently above Mother's headstone. Inspired by nature's dance, I took a deep breath and savored the aroma of tart lemons and honey that floated in the breeze. The air felt soft and comforting as if Mother Nature had paused to acknowledge my presence. I inhaled the delightful scent while dreaming of lemon tarts and pound cakes and pondering which bakery to visit. It was a toss-up between The Little Tart Bakery Shop and Flaky Not Flaky, within a mile of my mother and me. As I considered stopping by one on the way home, my mouth began to water.

"You know, Granny's close by," I said softly, my gaze rising to the graceful limbs of the magnolia swaying above us. Its branches reached out against the vast, blue sky as if refusing to allow any shadow to dim its beauty. The thought of my grandmother wrapped me in a comforting embrace. "And guess who's around the corner? Margaret Mitchell."

"Gone with the Wind" was our cherished classic, a film that held countless memories of laughter and warmth between us. Mother would often playfully declare that one day, far in the future, she'd rest near her favorite writer. "I'll be in high company," she'd say with a twinkle in her eye, and I'd laugh along, promising to bring Mrs. Mitchell flowers too. It feels more important now than ever to keep that promise.

Once a year, we'd gather to watch "Gone with the Wind," typically during the summertime. It was the perfect season to brew sun tea and wear big floppy hats indoors. As we watched, we fanned ourselves while playfully shouting phrases like, "I do declare" and "Fiddle-lee-dee," much to my father's eye-rolling dismay. The burning of Atlanta always brought tears to my mother's eyes.

"I thought I might find you here," a man spoke up, breaking the moment.

"It's Tuesday," I said, grumbling as I put on my sunglasses. It was easier to talk to Daddy without looking him in the eye.

My father stood at the edge of the blanket, his tall frame blocking the sunlight and casting a long, slender shadow over where I lay. The silver threads of his hair glinted in the light that passed through the magnolia tree above. Illuminated from behind, he seemed nearly celestial. He was also attired for the office, or in his situation, for church, looking very dapper in a charcoal suit paired with a light blue tie. I found myself smiling at the coordinated handkerchief placed in the breast pocket of Daddy's jacket, recalling how Mother frequently referred to him as "Mr. Debonair" when they were alone. At church, however, he was always Mr. Bennett or simply Pastor. His presence, once a source of comfort, now felt like a reminder of the void left by Mother's absence.

"Were you looking for me, Daddy?" I sank back onto my blanket, turning my gaze away.

Silence followed, and after a moment, I rolled over on my side, propping myself up on my elbow. Daddy's eyes wandered over the cemetery. Like most people, he had that look; a mix of appreciation and awe flashed through his eyes.

"Your mother loved magnolias."

"I think Momma likes it here," I said, looking around, though familiar with every bush, path, and bench. "Did you need me, Daddy?"

His eyes flashed as if he'd just remembered why he'd come. "They need us at the church. The congregation, that is. We're planting trees today, near the playground, in your mother's memory, and they'd like us there."

The church, a modest yet welcoming building, had always been a second home to us. The congregation, a diverse group of people, had been deeply affected by my mother's passing, and their efforts to honor her memory were both touching and overwhelming.

"What kind of trees?" I don't know why I asked. The question merely popped out as if the details would determine my attendance.

Daddy's Nordic blue eyes narrowed over me. "It's a kind gesture. We should be there." His words were soft, painfully weak.

Guilt flooded over me as I began to fold the blanket I'd been lying on.

"What are you planning to do with the old flowers?" he asked, shoving his hands into the front pockets of his sharply pressed suit pants.

"I've been drying them. I'm thinking about spreading some along Carter's Lake," I said, and I saw my father visibly tense over the words. His jaw tightened, and for a moment, I saw a flicker of pain in his eyes. It was as if the thought of parting with these dried remnants was too much to bear.

While it had been the first time we'd spoken about our family cabin on the lake since Mother's illness, I was aware Daddy had been shunning memories like he avoided alcohol—out of sight, out of mind. It seemed we were at an impasse; I wanted to talk about Mother. Daddy wanted to talk about God.

"Mrs. Rudabaker is organizing the event," Daddy continued, knowing my love for the kind woman who not only babysat me but also schooled me every Sunday, as she did all the children in the church. "You know, Maddy loved your mother, and she loves you."

"I'll be there," I said flatly.

"After the tree is placed, there will be a small prayer gathering in the main sanctuary." My father tried to sound casual, but I knew better; this was him requesting my presence.

I considered the idea briefly before saying, "I'll think about it." But my mind was already made up; I would not be attending any prayer service, and, in fact, I planned to escape right after planting the trees.

Daddy studied me, those sad eyes scanning my face, before saying, "Be angry at the world, Sam." His voice rang with a pain I'd never heard before, each word sadder than the one before as he continued, "Be angry at cancer, or the whole damned world, for all I care, but don't be angry with God. It won't help a thing, baby girl."

When I didn't respond, not even with a short retort, my father turned to head for the exit and, no doubt, the God he'd advocated for. I watched him as he walked away, shoulders drooping like a weight rested there. His silver fox head tipped ever so slightly as if the worry and grief that resided there were too heavy to bear. My heart sank over the sight of what had to be the loneliest man in the world and the knowledge that I was making it worse.

"I'm sorry, Momma." I looked down at the dried flowers still in my hand and cried.

CHAPTER ELEVEN

(The Pastor)

"And he will send his angels with a loud trumpet call, and they will gather his elect from the four winds, from one end of the heavens to the other."

— MATTHEW 24:31

"This must be a test," Richard muttered under his breath, grappling with the weight of his emotions as he lumbered along a winding path within the Oakland Park Cemetery. A test of faith or resilience? He didn't know. That question kept him up most nights. Well, that and his daughter's utter anger towards God, a rage born from the loss of her mother that turned his stomach when alone.

"What am I to do, Evelyn?" While faith told him she was happily in Heaven, unaware of the mess here on earth, he continued anyway. "I hope you're happy, honey." Richard's voice trembled as he walked, speaking to the love of his life, his partner in every sense of the word, now gone from this world.

While he found comfort in the understanding that Evelyn resided in Heaven, he needed—no, insisted—that something good should come from this tragedy, for Samantha's sake. He longed for an event, perhaps a miraculous healing or a profound spiritual experience, to reassure his daughter that God was always in control. Their grief would prove to be a worthy sacrifice for a greater purpose.

"Otherwise..." he said, his heart sinking as he stopped to slip a hand into his pocket, chest heaving a heavy sigh. "Sam may never come around."

He walked on, admiring the late afternoon sunlight as it filtered through the flowering dogwood trees overhead, casting shadows across the ground on his way to the serene resting place of his beloved wife.

Evelyn's final resting place; the words felt strange on his lips.

Because he was older than she, he always thought he'd go first, not Evelyn. Not his self-sacrificing, beautiful wife. Why had God not taken him instead? He would have gladly swapped places with her; she could have stayed and navigated this process better than he ever could, and...his daughter? Samantha would recover and, eventually, be happy.

The last thought halted his steps, and he pushed a shaky hand through his greying hair. Anger surged, not at God nor Samantha, but at life. The random injustices of the world. He might have cried if he hadn't felt so much resentment in that moment.

"I'll cry later," he said softly, emotion flushing his face.

He could barely hear the birds singing as he wrestled with a heavier thought. Did Sam wish it was him in that plot? Did he honestly believe that? Deep down, he knew this was only grief talking. It was true that Samantha had been closer to Evelyn—a natural bond for daughters, he believed—but she would never wish such a tragedy on anyone. Never.

He rounded the next corner and spotted Samantha by her mother's graveside.

"I thought I might find you here," he said, heart sinking at his daughter lying flat on her back beside her mother. An open wicker basket and a bouquet of flowers were arranged nearby as if they were about to have a picnic. It would have been an endearing scene if it hadn't looked so sorrowful.

When he reached the edge of the blanket, Sam opened her eyes.

"It's Tuesday," she said, pushing herself up from the patchwork quilt the Parks family had given her many Christmases ago. He forced a smile as his beloved daughter quickly adorned dark sunglasses and tilted her chin toward him. Like at the tender age of 12, Sam was back to hiding behind dark sunglasses whenever she felt anger, shielding herself from some preconceived judgment. The question was whether she was hiding from him or God.

While he didn't fully understand this behavior, he longed to tell her he understood. That he, too, felt a rage that cultivated a shameful spirit. But his daughter's generation often leaned toward impersonal communication—favoring a text over phone calls. Sam was no different; she was simply a product of her time.

"Did you need something, Daddy?" said his daughter as she flopped down, back flat to the blanket, and turned away her face.

I need my wife back! That's what he wanted to scream into the breeze. Instead, he crossed his arms over his dark suit jacket and shifted his gaze. He looked at the white blooms of an old magnolia tree above Evelyn's grave.

"Your mother loved magnolias," Richard said, his attention shifting to the neighboring graves, each adorned with colorful potted flowers that he assumed were favored by the souls remembered there. He felt torn between the desire to move on and the fear of forgetting, between the need to be strong for his daughter or crawl into bed for the remainder of the year.

"I think Momma likes it here." Sam's words jerked him back to the moment.

He wondered if Evelyn could have imagined the scene they were now forced to live as he stared at their daughter, seeing her as if for the first time. She looked so thin. Had she always been this thin?

"Did you need me, Daddy?"

When she asked again, he reluctantly brought up the topic of church and the tree that Mrs. Madeline Rudabaker—affectionately known as Maddy—had arranged on Evelyn's behalf. He noticed Sam's jaw tightening in defiance, a habit he had been trying to correct since she was five but had long since given up on.

"Mrs. Rudabaker has put a lot of effort into organizing the event," he explained as she sorted the dead leaves beside her into piles according to their level of dehydration. Then he noticed the fresh flowers in Evelyn's vase. "What will you do with the old flowers?"

"I've been drying them. I'm thinking about spreading some along Carter's Lake," was all she'd say, offering no details or invitation, and he knew better than to press.

The family cabin at Carter's Lake held some of their best memories: having lunch together by the water's edge, taking midnight walks with his wife after Sam had gone to bed, and countless other moments. It was painful to recall these times. He longed to forget, but he would always choose to remember.

"You know, Maddy loved your mother, and she loves you." He tried to guide his daughter back to the topic, such as the church event.

He could see the wheels turning in his daughter's mind, the anger so close to the surface that he could almost taste it. He hated watching Samantha struggle, her pain palpable in the air. But what baffled him even more was that she had faced troubles months before Evelyn's passing. It was a challenging time for everyone. In her final days, his wife revealed that their daughter had privately confessed to envisioning white lights on planes and in the hospital, reminiscent of the day they first heard the word "cancer."

He was unsure of how to process this revelation.

Given his disbelief in ghosts and aliens, the only option left was demons. The idea of a dark world fit with his faith, but it was also what he feared the most. His fear created a palpable tension in the air, adding to the uncertainty of their situation.

"I'll be there," Sam said flatly and slightly irritated.

He'd take what he could get.

CHAPTER TWELVE

(The Angel)

"Praise the LORD, you his angels, you mighty ones who do his bidding, who obey his word."

— PSALMS 103:20

Kalamazoo, Michigan. A place he never expected to find himself. As the taxi driver pulled up to Wings Stadium, a concert and convention center, he wondered how long before he'd master the angelic freeway. Since that night with Samantha months ago, his travel accuracy has been nothing to brag about. It seemed that anything he encountered—be it a book, a movie, or even a new food—would linger in his mind. For instance, after watching "Murder in the Hamptons" on a hotel TV with an overwhelming number of channels, he accidentally dropped in on a wedding reception in The Hamptons. Then there was the retirement party in India, inspired by the book "Eat, Pray, Love."

A small-town boy from Tupelo in India? Elvis laughed. His travel log had become quite extensive, thanks to his seventy percent expected accuracy. This meant that thirty percent of the time, he found himself in places he never intended to be, not in Memphis, Graceland, or any other significant location in his life. Now, he was here in the flesh and about to experience the chill of a Michigan spring. *I really need to do better.*

He had heard that winnowing, the process of angelic travel, was tricky. He just wished someone had told him that wherever an angel focuses their thoughts, that's where their body will travel—and as it turns out, this happens at stomach-churning speeds. This was another critical detail he would have liked to have known beforehand.

If he had been aware, he wouldn't have been randomly remembering April 26, 1977, a rare occasion when he had felt good on stage before his death. The sensation of being winnowed felt like being pulled through a vortex, with the world around him blurring into streaks of light and color.

"They call it the Angel Highway," he grumbled. *Whoever said the Archangel Gabriel lacked a sense of humor should have been shot.* He paused, brows burrowing over the purely human thought.

As he checked his pockets, hoping to find cash, he reassured himself that it could have been worse. Gabriel could have dressed him for summer, swapping the warm boots, knit hat, and jacket he wore now for shorts and a t-shirt.

"Yeah, that Gabriel is real funny," Elvis said, shaking his head as he examined his head-to-toe black outfit more thoroughly. *I look like a cat burglar!* "Be careful what you ask for, son." He suddenly quipped to the taxi driver. But the man merely narrowed his eyes in the rearview mirror as if to ask, *Haven't I seen you before?*

"Thanks, for the ride pal." Elvis cleared his throat, dropping cash onto the front seat as he stepped out into the 40-degree spring day. "Be safe now, you hear?"

He stood on the sidewalk with his hands buried in his pockets, watching the taxi drive away before turning his gaze to the aging building. The structure had seen better days; some roof shingles were rotting while others were missing entirely. Despite its worn appearance, a smile crept across his lips as memories of the antics on stage in Michigan flooded back to him.

He recalled the ecstatic women in the front row, eagerly reaching for kisses and scarves. He also thought about the playful pranks he pulled on his bandmates, like when he walked past the keyboard player in the middle of a song and unplugged his equipment. Everyone on the stage and in the audience laughed.

Chuckling at the memory and still standing in front of the old stadium, he gave it a slight bow. "Now, where should I eat?" He inhaled sharply, turning to face the horizon. In the distance, he spotted a building and felt confident that a restaurant must be nearby. After all, wherever there's work, there are workers on lunch breaks searching for food.

When his stomach growled, he shook his head in frustration. His stomach gurgled and rolled, driving him crazy as it demanded food—food and more food. He thought that perhaps his stomach was making up for lost time. It felt like all he'd done since he left Sam's side was drop in on strangers and eat.

With his wool hat pulled down around his ears, and his collar turned up, he set off to satisfy the hunger gnawing at his insides. Cars he had never seen before passed by, each one a different shape and size. The only car symbol he recognized was the Cadillac. A big, black Cadillac stopped at a red light, and he paused to look. The man driving the car glanced sideways in a quick evaluation, and Elvis grinned.

"That's a beauty of a car, friend!" he yelled loudly, concerned that the driver wouldn't hear him through the tank's heavy exterior.

The driver never looked back; the bulky vehicle sped off when the light turned green.

"You're a friendly fella." Elvis chuckled with amusement.

Although the sun was shining, it did little to warm the cool breeze that cut through his slacks like a knife through butter. He clenched his jaw, trying to stop his body from trembling. The angel Gabriel had been clear in a recent evaluation: "A fight is coming, and you don't have long to prepare." However, the specifics of this fight remained a mystery, a puzzle he was eager to solve. He was fighting to protect Samantha, but he still didn't understand why or what her role was in this conflict.

For the time being, he'd reacquaint himself with the body he had inhabited, as he would soon need to face Samantha again—eye to eye. He recalled the last time he had stood so close to this beautiful woman and realized that, at the very least, he would need to enhance his self-control skills before their subsequent encounter.

As Elvis quickened his pace, motivated by a persistent hunger and the cold breeze stinging his cheeks, a fast-food sign glowed like a beacon ahead. He looked upward and gave a thankful nod to the Almighty.

With each determined step, he reminded himself that it was just two more blocks. He only needed to walk two more blocks, and then he could sink his teeth into a juicy burger, indulging and relishing in as many as he could handle. Memories of his youth flooded back to him—a time when he once ate upwards of a dozen hamburgers in one sitting. Of course, he was only 19— a growing young man and the new leader of an entire teenage generation. Those were the days.

As he pushed open the restaurant's door, a quaint bell chimed, announcing his arrival. He paused a moment, taking in the scene around him. Five patrons occupied the black tables adorned with bright yellow tops, their attention primarily focused on their plates. A comforting hum of conversation filled the air.

In the far corner, a woman with salt-and-pepper hair, her features etched with the wisdom of her 70 years, caught his eye. She was sitting at a table flanked by two small children, likely her grandchildren. When their eyes met, he felt a chill run over him as the woman did a double take. He pulled the knit cap tighter around his head and went straight to the front counter, where a young man waited to take his order.

"Can I help you?" the high school-age boy asked, chewing a stick of gum vigorously.

Elvis sensed the woman's gaze from the corner when he said in a low tone, "I'll take three bacon cheeseburgers, please."

The young man stopped chewing his gum, his eyebrows lifting in shock at the order. Elvis began to fidget, unsure if it was due to the quantity of the order or the item.

"You do have bacon cheeseburgers, don't you, son?"

The boy looked behind Elvis as if looking for the missing entourage. "You want three burgers?"

"Make that five, with fries and a Pepsi." He smiled big.

"We don't have Pepsi."

Elvis frowned. "Okay, then make that a shake, vanilla will be fine."

When the young man left to fulfill his order, Elvis remained still, his palms flat against the counter. He could feel the woman's gaze burning into him from behind. Although her face wasn't familiar, he'd recognized the look in her eyes—a knowing glance that suggested he had sparked a memory for her. While it had been a while since he'd encountered that look of admiration, it was hard to forget. He only hoped she wouldn't discover the evading memory too soon. At least not before he could eat.

"Hey there, friend?" Elvis's voice rose to get the young man's attention. "Do y'all have a bathroom I can use?"

He didn't need to use the restroom but needed a moment. Following the direction pointed out to him, he walked toward the men's room, wanting some time to collect his thoughts and devise a plan in case things went wrong. The woman with dark eyes watched him intently as he passed by her, opened the door, and slipped inside.

A detergent scent filled the air as he approached the white ceramic sink and turned on the faucet with a twist. The sound of water filled the room, echoing softly against the grey-tiled walls. He paused momentarily, drawn to his reflection in the mirror above the sink. With a slight frown, he tilted his head to one side as if searching for a different perspective to unravel the mystery of his appearance. Those high cheekbones and pouty lips, familiar to him and the world, were bound to give him away. He knew it.

"Good, Lord," he called out to The Almighty, both in question and with a request. "I hope you're watching. This might go bad." He pressed his hand flat against his chest and adjusted his black t-shirt, which peeked out from beneath his jacket to reveal the phrase, 'Just do it.' *Just do what?* he wondered, turning his chin to the right to view his reflection from another angle.

"You can't stay in here all day," he told himself, then took a steadying breath, turned off the water, and walked towards the exit. "Leave the same way you entered. Concentrate on your destination."

He squeezed his eyes shut, picturing the first city that came to mind, in case he needed a quick escape. He could see the road parallel to the mighty river, the lighted bridge, and the old buildings in his mind's eye. When he flung open the door, he stumbled, nearly tripping over the tiny, bent woman who had been watching and waiting. He could have sworn her eyes flashed with a familiar love reminiscent of something he had seen on stage.

Holly hellfire, he almost said, but he caught himself and recovered, "I'm sorry, ma'am. Please excuse me."

"You're him, aren't you?" the woman said, leaning in closer and looking at his brown locks, which seemed to confuse her.

"I'm sorry, ma'am, but I'm late for an appointment." He squeezed past her, gently moving her body to the left of his.

"Why aren't you dead?" she asked flatly.

He glanced at the burgers stacked on a tray on the counter; the young man was waiting for him to return and pay for the food that still made his mouth water.

"Ma'am, I don't know who—" he began, but she interrupted.

"You should be ashamed of yourself, faking your death!"

His deep blue eyes widened, and he stammered, "I-I didn't..." before shutting his eyes. He thought of the one place dear to his heart and let go of his mind.

A wind rushed over him, making his body feel nimble, as light as particles in space. There was no pain, only the sensation of a breeze caressing his arms and legs, fracturing and reforming with every breath. One moment, he felt frantic, and the next calm. There was no fear—only the exhilarating freedom of movement, akin to the graceful Bassai dance in karate, which embodies the power and spirit needed to penetrate an enemy's fortress—or, in his case, time constraints. When the dizziness subsided, he felt solid ground beneath his feet and humidity beading his brow. Slowly, he opened his eyes to reveal...Beale Street.

Standing on the corner of Riverside Drive and Beale, a smile crept across his face. Elvis looked to his left at the dark, rolling Mississippi River, inhaling the earthy scent of soil and mud deep into his lungs. In the distance, he could see the bridge stretching over the harbor toward Mud Island and Arkansas beyond. Looking to his right, up Beale, he thought of Club Handy. It was once the hottest music spot in town. He had spent much time there enjoying the blues and making friends.

Home. He was home. The land of the Delta Blues, the king of cotton. How about that? His heart's desire had boldly led him back to Memphis. Graceland was only a short drive away, he mused as he walked up Beale Street, sweat dripping from beneath the stocking cap.

"I'll go there first," he said, walking with his hands deep in his pockets and his jacket zipped up to his chin. "Then I'll…" He stopped mid-sentence.

What would he do, exactly? Memphis wasn't where he was truly needed. While his heart had brought him here, Graceland wasn't where The Almighty had sent him. Samantha was his responsibility. Although he still had no idea what was happening or what was coming, he knew…

"I need to be in Atlanta," he said, his blue eyes sparkling with determination as he glanced around the bustling city and grinned. "Taxi!"

He sprinted across the street, where a couple stepped out of a cab as if ready to see the sights. "Can I borrow your ride?" He smiled big for the stunned tourists and thanked them, then slid into the cab and slammed the door.

"To the airport, please," Elvis said to the driver, waving at the couple as the car pulled away from the curb.

Leaning his head against the cool window, he closed his eyes tight, concentrating on the Bennetts—from the pastor to Mr. Big Boots and, at last, Samantha—his Sam. He kept her likeness vividly in his thoughts as a familiar wind softly enveloped him. Quickly, he slammed that door mentally shut.

For now, he'd fly. *Thank you very much*. He thought and gave a chuckle, to which the driver glanced up at him from inside the rearview mirror.

"I-I'm a little nervous. It's been a while since I'd last flown."

The young man nodded. "You've been here before then?"

"A long time ago," Elvis spoke softly as the car picked up speed and merged onto the freeway.

They weren't on the highway long before he saw the Elvis Presley Blvd, Graceland W Brooks Rd exit sign. His heart sank as they passed it, longing surging deep in his very bones. His need to go home was so strong that his hands began to shake. He clamped his palms together and squeezed until it hurt, anything to break the spell.

"What airline would you like, sir?"

"American Airlines, " he answered without thinking. It wasn't Samantha's airline, but one he knew well. He'd flown to D.C. on American once, when he visited President Nixon in the White House. His eyes sparkled with the memory.

When the hometown airport came into view, Elvis sat up straighter. The years of flying his Convair 880 jet, lovingly coined the Lisa Marie, in and out of this airport came flooding back. Those last-minute trips to Denver for the best Gold Loaf, a peanut butter and jelly sandwich he loved, and too many trips to Hawaii or Vegas to even count all washed over him at that moment. He didn't want to leave. He wanted to stay and enjoy Memphis, his town. His long-lost friend.

"Here you go, sir. That'll be thirty dollars, " the driver said as he pulled the cab to the curb, stopping under a sign that read departures.

Elvis stuffed his hand in his pants' never-ending money pocket and prayed. When he felt paper bills rustling against his fingertips, he smiled.

"Here you go, friend, " he said, handing him the money. He didn't have to look; only fifty-dollar bills were in his pockets. "Keep the change."

"Thank you!" The driver smiled as he pulled away.

Turning, Elvis took a wide, hands-on hip stance, eyeballing the entrance with great skepticism. While in the spirit, he had flown with Samantha a million times, following her through airports worldwide. He knew how the modern day of flying worked, with all its shoes off or leaving them on commands, the pat-downs, and the handheld metal detectors. The smoking and the no-smoking sections were a thing of the past, which was not an issue of his time; he understood it all.

"Hold on, honey. I'm coming," Elvis said with a sly smile as he stepped into a new beginning—a journey that would take him to Atlanta, a city filled with new challenges.

Despite uncertainty about the future, Elvis remained steadfast in his faith in the Lord Almighty, who held everything in His hands. Together, they would overcome whatever challenges lay ahead—today, tomorrow, and forever.

AUTHORS NOTE

"Write what you know." I'd heard it said a million times before. And as it turns out, it was the best advice I was ever given. I'm not a seasoned writer or an award-winning author. But over the last 15 years, I've experienced a deep closeness with my readers, a personal connection that all writers pray for. They came to me, sharing their dreams and stories, not just about a man known the world over by only one name—ELVIS—but also about their own lives. Why? What had I done that I should be so blessed with a reader base so early in my career? My first story, *Eternal Flame*, is fiction or Elvis-fiction as we like to call it in the Elvis world. I can assure you it's not the preferred reading material for the average Elvis fan. It's not even a popular genre for most publishers. What sells in this niche are stories written by those who knew Elvis Presley. Truth or variations of the truth is what sells books. So, why did I bother?

The Elvis world is flooded with "stories" every year. And as an Elvis fan myself, I knew it would be hard for a fiction writer to fit in. Bottom line, Elvis fans like the "real" Elvis. We don't want a shadow of the man. We want to know what made the true man tick. But because he's been gone for more than forty years, new stories are hard to come by. Many biographies have been repeated, rearranged, and/or reworded so many times over that one can't help but feel skeptical whenever a new book hits the shelf. After all, nobody likes to spend $26.00, or more, for a hardback. only to discover they've read it all before!

I set out to write what *I* craved as a fan, a fantasy that felt real to me. I wrote *my* relationship with the legacy that is Elvis Presley, what my heart knew to be true. And before I knew it, Elvis fans around the world slowly joined the journey. Turns out, my story was their story. Nobody was more surprised than me.

Soon it became clear that readers were drawn to not only the characters but to what was real inside the story. They were drawn to the struggle and bottom line—they could relate. Inside these written words of honesty, they saw a piece of their own life. Somehow by bringing my own pain into the light, I drew closer to my audience. We created a bond.

Every writer needs a reader! After all, what's the point of writing if nobody reads it?

So, my advice to you is this. If you're a writer, no matter the level, and you're struggling to connect with your fan base, take heart. Let me encourage you to find just one pulsating truth inside the fiction you're writing. Express it honestly, even if it brings you great pain. Readers are waiting for stories that move them. They want to connect with you, with someone. Don't be afraid.

And if you're an avid reader, let me just thank you for all your time and devotion. Without you waiting to read what comes next, storytellers like me would be truly lost. *You* are the reason we write. Thank you.

Patricia Garber, co-host of Blue Suede Connection, and CEO of Jungle Room Press, a small indie publishing company dedicated to the angelic quality inside every story, has donated author royalties to charities since 2007. While in the past, the charities were often the programs Elvis himself approved of while alive, for 2024 and 2025, donations from The Angelic Saga will go to The Elvis Presley Charitable Foundation. **Readers can contact Patricia Garber at eternflame@yahoo.com or follow her at the links below.**

https://www.facebook.com/theangelicsaga

https://www.amazon.com/stores/author/B006T3O61Q?ingress=0&visitId=6f448915-df4f-4e87-9bc3-4bcf56fe53c6&ref_=ap_rdr

ETERNAL FLAME

PATRICIA GARBER

CHAPTER ONE

Dear Diary, it's been a long time since we last spoke. I need help, and I don't know where to turn anymore. I have made some bad choices in my life so far, but the mess I've managed to get into this time tops them all. What does a girl do when she falls in love with something that doesn't belong to her? She knows this cannot go on, but the idea of living without it seems worse than the repercussions of keeping it. Is there anyone or anything out there that cares for the suffering of the brokenhearted?

"Honey, could you show me where you keep your coffee?" I could hear his rich familiar voice, giving real question to my sanity, as he called out to me. "You're out."

As though mesmerized, I followed the invisible path of his intoxicatingly masculine scent that pulled me through the house into the kitchen. No man had the right to smell so good at such great distances. I found myself analyzing his fragrance, his essence. What was that smell anyway? It was like a great cologne, unlike anything the most talented designer could create, mixed with the natural scent of a fresh spring rain. Only nature could create a bouquet so clean and crisp. I stifled a deep sigh as I looked at him, standing there ready for the day. He was leaning casually against the counter, watching his new world outside my window, unaware I'd entered the room. I caught myself almost envying how he made looking good seem all so effortless. He was a perfect picture of a real man. Every hair accounted for, in its ideal place, and a face of an angel. It hit me then that I'd never find another like him. The history-proven fact was that there never has been another man like him. This undeniable awareness allowed fear to needle its way into my heart. If I fell in love with this man, that surely meant loneliness in my future.

I wasn't aware he drank coffee, I realized as he turned toward me, morning sunlight catching the sparkle off his famously blue eyes.

Just look at that beautiful face I'm now sharing my days with. How did I get into this situation? He needs to go back now, before I can't let him. It seems like a lifetime ago when this whole mess got started, and yet it's only been days since he stepped into my life. But I know it's only a matter of time before he steps back out. I still remember the day that I now call the first day of my renewed life, when my coworker and travel buddy Heather Dawson called with an offer that started it all.

"Hope you're calling because you have something wickedly fun to propose..." I said into the phone without even bothering to say hello. I was eager to hear any schemes for new adventures she might have up her sleeve.

Heather and I were both flight attendants for a major airline and had been friends since we started our professions at the age of nineteen. Our bond grew early out of our mutual love of both travel and the airline benefits that allowed us to frequently do so—anywhere, anytime.

"Samantha, do I have a trip of a lifetime to offer you."

I held my breath, anticipating a string of thrilling details yet to be shared. Traveling with Heather was always a curious mix of expectation and trepidation.

"Whatcha got?" I said as I took a seat in the chocolate-suede recliner next to the phone station.

I stretched my long legs out in front of me and gave in to the comforts a leisurely chat can bring. I was never more aware of how few people I now had in my life with whom to share such an easy conversation. I remembered how my desire to be interwoven with family and friends had brought me back to my hometown of Atlanta, Georgia, in the first place. Things had been so good in the beginning. I smiled in remembrance of how my phone would ring impatiently with invitations to Sunday dinners that my mother was sure I did not want to miss. I couldn't believe it had been two years since cancer had overcome her and swept her away from me.

Heather's voice hummed in my ear as I struggled against a storm of bad memories insidiously working its way into my mind. The questioning tone of her voice abruptly brought me back from the dark place I was lingering.

"Sam, are you listening to me? Boston in the spring..." she said.

My focus flickered as I tried get back into our easy banter. I had no idea how many of the details I'd missed, but the East Coast sounded fabulous. In my head, I was already packing as I contemplated my favorite place to be during the changing of the seasons. No matter if it's winter to spring or summer to fall, I'd never been disappointed when visiting the east. I loved how the crisp morning air would grudgingly give way as the sun came out to warm my bones, an unavoidable reminder that summer was fast approaching.

"Boston? Sounds great. Outside of the airport, I've never seen Boston," I said.

Instantly, I began thinking about digging out my mother's camera. She had loved to capture the changes in nature that were so often taken for granted in everyday living.

"Yep, me either. I'd like to make a drive to Salem, too..." Heather paused, then cautiously added, "... if you don't mind."

My experience in Boston might have been limited, but I knew enough about the area and my friend to know this would be another stop on her long list of paranormal destinations.

"It's just one night, Sam." Heather continued, trying to sell the idea as I listened silently.

"Well, one night I could probably handle," I sighed.

I squirmed involuntarily in my chair at the thought of exploring the supernatural and made a mental note not to share any photos with my Baptist-preacher daddy. Not unless I had time for a passionate sermon about trusting God to open your eyes to such things on judgment day and not before.

"That's my girl!" she exclaimed. "See you tomorrow."

As she hung up, I feared I'd gotten into more than I could handle.

My mind shifted gears as I lugged my favorite faded black suitcase out from my crowded closet. It looked dreadful, but every single scratch and ding was a visible reminder of past adventures. Packing for any trip, work or pleasure, was always a time-consuming event for me. As I dug through my wardrobe and looked for something striking, I stumbled across my favorite yellow sundress. If only it was warmer on the East Coast now. I loved how I looked in that dress, so feminine and petite with just a hint of sexual promise in its plunging neckline. I imagined a good bra might help rally up a little more cleavage. Heat rushed to my cheeks from my surprising audaciousness.

Reluctantly, I decided the sundress would have to wait. I picked out a few sweaters and light jackets that would be more practical for early spring weather. I held a blue sweater up to my face and examined myself in the mirror. With my chestnut hair, a gift from my beautiful mother, and the soul-piercing blue eyes of my father, I was aware that men found me attractive. At least until they deemed me unapproachable, usually within the same heartbeat. My initial shyness with strangers, though not my true self, didn't help matters. I vowed this trip to not succumb to that bashfulness that always comes over me when I meet someone new. Unwelcome, uncontrollable, and totally unlike my true self, it worked in cruel tandem with the maddeningly stale cycle that was my current social life.

I threw down the blue sweater and reached for a white one instead. As I examined my wardrobe change in the mirror, I studied my flaws and celebrated my advantages. I'd always wished to be a more voluptuous woman, but was given a petite frame instead. I sighed in resignation. I knew I had no choice but to do the best with what I'd been given. Thirty was looming over me, ready to lower the hammer on my single twenties, and I wondered how much longer I'd be alone. The race with my internal clock was beginning to exhaust me. A ringing phone broke my trance, and I raced to catch it. "Hello," I answered cheerfully, pleased that for once I had beat that answering machine to the punch.

"This is going to be so much fun. We should be there before noon, and we'll head straight for Salem."

I smiled as Heather's excitement overrode her phone etiquette.

"Sam?"

"Who is this?" I sternly teased. I marveled at all of the pent-up energy that, as always, would keep her up the night before a trip.

"What?" Heather said, confused. Never would it occur to her I might not have known it was her calling.

"I'm only kidding." I laughed. "I'm ready and willing, Captain."

"Well, good, because we're on the early morning flight, and you know what that means..." she said. Had it been in person, the statement would have come with a wink and a nudge.

To Heather, all business travelers, especially of the male sort, took that early morning flight to the East Coast. Independently single and also in search of her soul mate, the possibilities seemed endless.

"I wonder if we'll get into first class," she pondered out loud.

"Yes, I'm aware of your early morning philosophy." I tried to sound as excited as she was, but I hated flying that early.

"You *are* leaving the 'man-repeller' at home this time?" She asked me accusingly.

"Don't worry. I don't have it on today." I held back a sigh of impatience. My treasured Elvis souvenir absolutely was going with me, just not around my neck.

"Good, because you remember our last trip..."

There it was, I thought as I rolled my eyes. I wondered how long before she'd mention her displeasure with our last adventure. I'd bought my lucky charm several years ago during a trip to Memphis. The last time Heather and I flew, it became a conversation piece for two men we had met onboard our flight. They did not find it as precious as I did. After some Elvis-bashing by the two gentlemen, my patience, to quote a phrase, "left the building."

"It wasn't my fault those guys were such jerks." I crossed my free arm around my stomach, tense at the memory.

Exasperated with the subject, I tried to convince her I was not at fault. Unfortunately, their lack of manners and complete lack of understanding had quickly led to an unpleasant and abrupt ending to what Heather had hoped to be a promising connection.

"Why do you always have to wear it when you fly?" She demanded.

"Because it comforts me."

I grew tired of explaining to everyday folk the reasons behind the perfectly normal habits of a true Elvis fan. I've been one since I was eight years old, and nothing was going to change now.

"You're so defensive where he's concerned, I swear, Sam." Heather was losing steam on the argument. She knew she couldn't fight me.

"Well, maybe so, but I'm not leaving it behind." I insisted. "But for you, I'll put it in my pocket so there's no worries."

I was not beyond compromising, but I never flew without my good-luck charm, and I wasn't starting now.

"Good, I'll meet you at the airport first thing in the morning. Wait until you see the books I found about Salem." With that, she promptly hung up.

I stood there and laughed at the dial tone humming in my ear. *She'd forgotten to say good-bye again,* I thought as I hung up and returned to the chore of packing. With hand on hip, I stared at my open bag as if waiting for its assistance to tell me what items I'd forgotten.

After a bit more inventorying, I finally accepted this was the best I was going to do. I closed up my bag and left it strategically placed by my front door. I had been known to walk right out the house in an early morning haze with no bag in hand. My clever planning pleased me, and I smiled all the way back to my bedroom. As I slipped off my light robe and pink bunny slippers, I stretched my arms out into the warm air that the ceiling fan kept circulating above my head. *It's already so hot, and it's only spring,* I thought as I plopped down on my bed. I yawned big, grabbed my down comforter, and banished it to the end of the bed frame.

I reached to the top of my bedside reading stack for the novel that I'd been told was a must-read. I adjusted my pillow and settled back into a mountain of feathers. Pleased with my comfortable arrangement, I paused to look at my diary lying untouched on the nightstand. Cynically I glared at it and noticed the dust now collecting over its paisley stamped leather cover. I hadn't touched it since my mother's passing. It looked so out of place amongst its immaculate surroundings.

Sighing, I rolled over onto my back, relaxed and ready for the good read I'd been looking forward to all evening.

However, satisfying the need for an entertaining diversion quickly began to fade after just a few lines. My arms grew tired of holding sweet pages of distraction, and the comfort of sleep began to consume me. I dropped the book onto the empty pillow beside me and drifted off. A dusty diary full of memories would haunt my dreams.

I woke up startled by my alarm at 4:00 the next morning. As it screamed throughout my bedroom, I found myself regretting that I'd agreed to catch that first flight with Heather. I dragged myself up into a wobbly stance, and my body fought against the idea of rising before the sun was up. My stomach flipped as I headed for my slippers and some hot coffee. I coaxed myself down the hallway to the slap-slap of pink bunny feet on the hardwood floor. My cautious steps only faltered when I jumped in surprise as the phone shrieked in the early stillness.

"Yes."

"Hey there, you're up. Good." Heather's energetic voice didn't even give hint to the fact she'd most likely not slept a wink.

"Yep. Jumping for joy. I'm up."

"Yes, and you sound so cheerful, too." Heather said, laughing at my misery.

"This is the best I can do at four in the morning."

"I'm sure that'll improve with coffee. Just called to make sure you were up. See you at the airport." And with that, she was gone again.

I vowed to seriously speak to her about this hanging up business as I dropped the phone back into its cradle.

* * *

I didn't fully wake up until I pulled into the airport parking lot. As if someone clicked on my internal light switch, I was finally aware of my surroundings. I must have driven the whole way on autopilot again, which wasn't a comforting thought. As if I had some kind of honing device implanted in my very bones, I migrated here like a bird in the clouds headed for southern climate. I didn't bother to lecture myself about unsafe road habits, as that never seemed to help. Instead, I raced to meet Heather at the main ticket counter, as she'd requested.

Heather and I quickly advanced to the gate without having to think through the airport's paces—this part was just another day in our lives. I had to remind myself this was a pleasure trip and not one for work. Like all good and prepared passengers, we had ample time before our flight to inspect the little shops that can ruin a budget even before the trip begins. After acquiring some high-priced snacks, we returned to our gate and blended in with the rest of the waiting crowd. I sat in silence and observed the buzzing energy of my fellow travelers. Some lingered around the check-in counter, determined to be the first in line. Others sat and pretended not to care, all the while keeping a watchful eye out for a gate agent's arrival. I snickered to myself as I considered this ritual was much like a strategic military movement. Hundreds of travelers kick off their adventures simultaneously with the boarding instructions that guide all alike to their respective seats. Only once seated does everyone on board have strict orders to begin their vacations.

I shook my head at my own imagination and turned my attention to the books Heather had brought about Salem's infamous history. With its population now standing at more than 40,000 and rising, Salem had risen dramatically from its small-village past of legendary acts of cruelty that are still discussed in history classes today. Goose bumps rose up on my arms as I was reminded of how the quaint beginnings of Salem in 1626 degenerated into the witch-hunts, trials, and burnings at the stake of the accused.

"This town sounds intense and scary," I admitted as I drug my eyes away from the artist's depiction long enough to look up at Heather.

"That was a long time ago. It should be interesting to see what it's become now." Heather's eyes never left the magazine she'd found discarded in the boarding lounge.

I narrowed my eyes to better examine the object of her interest. I peeked at the issue date and chuckled. I'd read that same edition while on the job at least three times last week out of sheer boredom. Just as I was about to make a sarcastic comment about how she might be spending her down time on duty, the gate agent made his imperious arrival. He wasted little time before starting in with the boarding announcements, and we stepped into line with the first class passengers bound for the East Coast. While I assumed Heather was contemplating who might be worthy of a good conversation during flight, I thought more about sleep and yawned.

I looked around casually at this morning's first-class travel mix. Predictably, it consisted mostly of businessmen who importantly carried black briefcases and sat in front to escape the woes of coach class. But there was one lone traveler standing with a big smile and too many carry-on bags who caught my eye. I had her pegged within five seconds as a first-time, first-class traveler. She was about my age and certainly seemed as friendly as she could be. She stood excitedly behind me in line.

"I've never flown in first class before," she said as she tapped me on my shoulder to get my attention.

"Oh? Well, there's a first time for everything," I offered with a weak smile.

"The alcohol is free, right?" she asked me as she adjusted a large, pink floppy hat. I would have been willing to bet she wore quite often.

"Yes, it is. But if they run out, ask her," I said and pointed in Heather's direction. "She probably has a stash of minis with her right now."

"What?" Heather said, sensing she'd become part of the conversation.

"This is my first time," the excited woman told Heather.

"Congratulations." Heather said and forced a smile as she turned back around.

I chuckled and imagined Heather's eyes rolling back inside her head over my new friend's exuberance. I liked her, right down to her plastic gardening shoes that matched that pink, droopy hat. She had flare, and I applauded her for being her true self. Whatever that really was, I was not sure.

PATRICIA GARBER

Our flight was on time and uneventful, just the way a flight should be. As expected, Heather chatted with the man in front of us, and I slept the whole way to Boston, only to be awakened when the landing gear again touched ground. I stretched and thought how a nap on a plane is the best way to get from point A to point B in the blink of an eye. Like I imagined time travel to be, a flight could be over just shortly after it started.

As we deplaned, Heather and I felt at home in the middle of the noisy crowd at the gate. After I made quick goodbyes to my new friend, we quickly moved through the terminal. We rolled our trusty carry-on bags and exchanged smiles as we sailed past a tense crowd at baggage claim. Before long, we had stepped up to a rental car counter, and a handsome young man ran us through the ritual. We cut him short when he got to directions, and instead headed straight for our adventure. We were well-traveled, why would we find Boston any different to navigate than most large cities?

Heather guided our rental car out from the garage and into the spring sun, still low in a pale eastern sky. The air was crisp and the sun warm on our windows as we jumped onto the freeway that would lead us to Salem. Heather weaved into the hectic traffic, coaxing our rental car into wide lanes full of locals rushing off to their appointments for the day. I marveled at how quickly drivers had to think to make an exit or miss other drivers trying to do the same. Heather loved to drive fast, but I could see her fingers turning white on the steering wheel as our speed escalated. I gripped the sides of my seat in fear. My stomach began to turn.

"You know, it would be okay if we got there in one piece," I said as she weaved in and out of traffic, which was actually going too slow for her taste.

"I've got it under control. This traffic is slower than the outskirts of Arkansas, 'cause Yankees can't drive," she laughed.

As Heather made a move into the right lane to avoid a slower driver, I squinted disbelievingly through a sun-blurred windshield. I sucked in my breath as I saw that our lane was quickly narrowing to a close with no room to merge. As if I was driving, I glanced over my left shoulder at the solid line of traffic that moved tightly by us. My heart began to race as I again looked forward. The end of the lane was coming fast with what looked like construction barrels blocking us from even using the shoulder. I started to yell my standard alarm.

"Heather, Heather, Heather, Heather!" I screamed, as if her name alone was warning enough.

"I got it, I got it, I got it!"

Everything slowed to one-quarter time as Heather's foot hit the brake. Her right arm came across my chest, like a mother protecting her child. Her well-intentioned gesture was no match for the sheer force of my body as I hurled toward the car's dash. Despite Heather's foot still buried on the brake, our car plowed headlong through the blockade. Orange water-filled barrels splattered their load in our wake. I dimly registered the thud of my forehead hitting the dash before I fell back into my seat.

After who knows how much time had passed, I realized we'd come to a stop. With my head pounding, I sat back and watched the spots float around in front of my blurred eyes. Are we okay? Is the rental okay? I looked over at Heather, who was secure in her seatbelt and staring at the never-ending flow of traffic that couldn't be bothered with such trifle things as an accident.

"You okay?" To speak was debilitating, and I winced at the pain. Already I was sure everything was going to hurt for days to come.

"They didn't even stop," said Heather, not quite focused on our immediate well-being.

Just as I was about to point out the miracle of our survival, I realized she was absolutely right. Not one car had even slowed, much less actually stopped. I found myself looking around in earnest, thinking that surely someone would stop eventually. It was as if nobody even noticed us as they continued down the freeway. Had we crashed right through the space-time continuum? Could people today really be so heartless?

We hadn't been in Boston but an hour, and already we'd had a serious mishap. I was beginning to wonder if this wasn't a bad sign that would follow us throughout the trip.

"They must notice that we're in one piece," I tried to offer up for comfort.

"Your head!" Heather's eyes widened as she pointed toward my already pounding cranium.

"Am I bleeding?" I reached up and with one touch felt a rush of pain between my eyes.

"No, but you're going to have a huge bump." She leaned forward to inspect my unsightly development. "I'm guessing that could teach anyone about seat belts."

"Why, thank you for all of your concern, friend," I said and tried to match her sarcastic tone. "Shall we get off the side of the road?"

Considering our rocky start on the Massachusetts freeway system, I counted us lucky that the car not only started, but also went on to transport us to our destination.

Soon Heather eased our now rattling car into the small town of Salem. My head was pounding less, but my hands continued to shake involuntarily. Heather's knuckles regained color as she loosened her grip on the steering wheel. Even she was glad to see the diminished traffic that downtown Salem brought. The slower pace eased my flustered nerves as well, though I was sure I would at least need some aspirin before the day was over.

The courtyards in the center of town had a historic feel of another period. Even the businesses had facades that harkened back to the town's historical beginnings. I admired the detail work in the construction of the faded red-brick buildings and narrow roads. A horse-drawn carriage in this town would not have surprised me at all.

All too soon, we were reminded of Salem's dark history as we passed the Witch Dungeon Museum at the center of town. Posters on the front of the building advertised the displays inside of the torture devices and dungeons of that period. I shuddered at the lack of reverence for those who suffered—just come on in and see the artifacts. The invitation was as open as one would offer to give a tour of their home. The building looked dark and evil to me with its shadowy doorways and iron guarded windows.

As we continued on, I noticed the local youth, lounging on benches in the local graveyards as if they were in a park. They chatted casually while sipping designer coffees, sitting amongst the dead in customary tranquility.

"Did you see that? They're hanging out in the graveyards like it's the mall."

Heather looked the direction I was pointing, but didn't reply.

"That'll be the day." I said.

As was my travel assignment, I continued to read directions as Heather took the final turn down a narrow gravel driveway. Our battle-worn car creaked to a grateful stop in front of a beautiful Victorian-era bed and breakfast. Relieved to get out of the vehicle that almost took our lives, I stretched as Heather opened the trunk.

The Crescent Inn was a stately two-story home that had been restored to its original 1906 condition. I marveled at the smallest details in hand-carved wood trim around the windows. We walked up front stairs that creaked with age, but I noticed had been newly painted. The front door was unusually tall and opened into a cozy lobby with maroon velvet high-back chairs and couches of the period stationed around a large stone fireplace. I marveled at a lion's head that was chiseled out of stone, much like something seen in an old horror movie. It was gothic meets Victorian, right before my eyes.

The deep-brown wooden floors groaned as we approached a grand mahogany check-in counter. Behind it was our tiny, bent hostess, her frail body in contrast with the huge piece of lumber she hid behind.

A stubby pencil was tucked into her short silver hair. She acknowledged us with a welcoming smile.

"Hello, ladies, how can I help you?" She asked courteously.

"We have a reservation for Dawson," Heather said.

"One moment, please." She turned away to thumb through a file where reservations were kept the old-fashioned way, on hand-written slips stored alphabetically.

"Take your time, Rose," Heather said, using the name on our hostess' time-worn nametag pinned to her shirt. Rose only smiled at Heather's forward nature.

As we waited, I wandered to the other side of the room. Heather finished the business of checking us in as I stopped and lingered over photos of a family posing in front of this grand house. The pictures hung two-by-two on walls that were covered in cream-colored flowered wallpapered. I had to lean in to see through the dingy color of time threatening to overcome the photos that displayed discouraged faces. The captured posed unnaturally. I imagined from their determination to tolerate the photo technology of that period. My eye followed around the frames' dark edges of hand-crafted wood and fell still upon an engraving that read "Haunted Home, 1906."

I shook my head as I started to piece together why Heather had chosen these accommodations: this catered perfectly to her love of ghosts. I snickered thinking what she might actually do if she really had a true paranormal experience. I, on the other hand, would be just fine if I never had one. My train of thought was broken when I heard Rose address Heather, apparently finishing up with her duties.

"Ms. Dawson, our famous room eight is ready for you a bit earlier then normal, if you ladies would like to get settled in now?"

I returned to Heather's side. She had to have felt my eyes burning a hole through her. She pretended to not feel it as she signed the final paperwork without making any eye contact.

"Thank you, Rose." Heather said and grabbed her bag, smirking slightly at my irritation she headed for the stairs leading us to our "famous room."

"What exactly is so famous about room eight, Heather?"

"Now, Sam, it's not as bad as you're imagining," she tried reasoning with me. "The room just has a history of being a tad haunted, and I thought since we were in town, we'd get its full effect."

The last time I'd gone along with one of Heather's ghost outings, we ended up in some old hotel in the middle of Arkansas.

"You seem to forget Arkansas."

"Sam, the medium in that hotel told you the ghosts were not hostile," she reminded me defensively.

"You don't find it odd at all that we stayed in a hotel that had a medium as regular staff?" I said and crossed my arms defiantly.

"There was no harm done, Sam." Heather said. "It was all in good fun."

Heather and I did not share the same upbringing that had formed our adult beliefs. Heather was from a wealthy Alabama family that welcomed new ideas and other beliefs. Consequently, Heather was open to experiencing all things with no fear. Conversely, my middle-class, preacher's kid upbringing led by the much more strict Pastor and Mrs. Bennett of Georgia was less flexible. However, our respect for each other's differences was what made our friendship work. That's not to say it was easy, but it was worth it.

"You know I prefer to leave these things where they belong." I told her. I fully believed what my daddy used to say about the other side. It's on the other side for a reason, and it's God's business to handle, not mine. "Sam," Heather tried to reason with me. "We've done this before."

"Yes, but it's different now. I'd never known anyone who had ... passed." My voice lowered in embarrassing emotion, and I almost couldn't finish.

Heather's eyes softened as she considered what I'd just said. Without a word, she headed back to the huge mahogany desk to explain to Rose why we couldn't stay. In compassion, Rose called around until she found us another room in a newer, un-haunted hotel nearby.

After another regrettable loading of our rental car, we pulled into a more modern hotel and quickly got checked in. The front desk manager, a man in his forties working in an environment less inspiring then the last, advised us we had an hour before our room would be ready. Meanwhile, Heather had spotted some shops across the street from our new hotel, so we headed out on foot to soak in some local color and flare.

The sun was high in the new spring sky. The apple trees were in bloom and displayed vibrant colors of pink amongst dark green foliage. Whether on the West or the East side of our country, one cannot beat the show Mother Nature puts on with every tree in bloom. I paused to take in the golden sun shining warmly on my face, enticing me to kick off my shoes and walk barefoot in a nearby park. Reluctantly, I abandoned the notion and instead chose to follow the ever-focused Heather into the first tourist shop she spotted.

The endless display of trinkets in one of these stores was enough to make anyone shop on autopilot. I stopped at the first display rack of key chains, as there was too many to really look at them all, and wondered if anyone actually collected them for travel memories. It was only in Memphis, surrounded with everything Elvis, that a store like this made any sense to me. I chuckled at my clearly biased opinion. Key chains and refrigerator magnets seem to be this store's specialty.

I was just about to suggest we go somewhere else when I noticed Heather staring out the window in the back of the store. I assumed she was bored and called out to her that we should move on. As I approached her, I noticed what had caught her eye.

Mystic Books. The bright red sign drew Heather like a proverbial moth to a flame. Although the store was clearly open, the sign was the only beacon to signal visitors to its tucked-away location on a side cobblestone street. It seemed hidden away like a gem that only the locals new about. Its location struck me as peculiar as I realized it was only visible from the nick-knack store where we stood. The buildings around it appeared to be empty but available for lease—no doubt because of location, they would stay that way for some time.

"Strange, it seems hidden almost," I mentioned, puzzled.

We left the first shop to walk around to the bookstore. As we approached, I could see another smaller advertisement: *Fortunes told and sold inside.* Sold? I had never seen such an offer, and I will admit I was intrigued.

Without hesitating, Heather ventured in and left me standing outside the frosted privacy doors. I quickly followed and was greeted by the sound of an entrance bell and the overwhelming sight of books stacked from the floor to the ceiling. The aroma of burning candles smelled like lavender and weakly masked the odor of molding paper. *My mother loved that scent*, I thought as I lingered in the entrance, unsure of my purpose or direction. I stretched my neck to look around, but could not spot my friend anywhere. She was already lost amongst the many books.

While I decided which way to go, I noticed a blue line on the hardwood floor. My eyes clung in hesitation to the painted floor marker that yearned for me to follow it. The idea that direction was needed to keep from getting lost inside the maze was intimidating enough to keep me cemented in my spot.

"Heather?" I whispered, unwilling to move.

I had no idea whom I might disturb but in a place like this, anyone could be in here. I waited and played with the buttons of my light spring jacket. No response came back from within the rows of books.

Small, crudely handwritten signs marked each isle's specialty. A shiver ran down my back at the one before me that read *spells and potions*. For the second time that day, I was again uncomfortable. Even if God and I were not on speaking terms, I had always believed

He was watching, even when I was a child. God had especially been ratting me out to my father my whole life. I never knew what I feared more, God's wrath or my father's, and I was raised to dread the wrath of both. As a child, I always ran to my mother to hide from their assumed opposing judgment against me. I often wondered if that is why God took her from me. Was he trying to flush me out from all of my hiding places?

Just as I proceeded to move, I heard a book hit the floor, and profanity soon followed.

"Shit, shit, shit!"

"Heather?" I again whispered.

"What are you whispering for? Damn it, my foot!"

I followed a steady stream of vulgarity and found my friend a row away. Seated on the dirty floor, she was inspecting her foot. I noticed her open toed sandals had been thrown aside in haste. The massive dusty novel that was responsible for her discomfort sat binder side up, too dirty for me to make out it's title.

"Dropped a book on your foot, did you?" I have always found humor in the obvious.

"No, I did not! I wasn't touching that book, it just fell off the shelf." Heather didn't look up from her throbbing limb.

"Hmm, well maybe our hotel ghost followed us here?" I offered.

"I'm in real pain here, Sam, do you mind?"

Though Heather was always the brave one, she could not handle the smallest amount of physical discomfort. Pain and dirt were Heather's enemies. I held back a giggle and inspected the dirt that now clung to Heather's once white posterior. This was not the time to point out the condition of her favored Capri pants.

"Sorry, you just look so funny down there."

Heather briskly stood up, swiping at long blonde hairs that clung to her face. She brushed herself off and took a moment to inventory her condition. Obviously not finding the event as funny as I had and satisfied nothing was broken, she returned to the business at hand.

"Did you see the sign coming in?" Heather quickly changed the subject.

"You mean 'fortunes told and sold'," I replied cautiously. I could already guess where this was going.

"Isn't that mysterious? I've never seen anything like it."

"Sounds like a hook for tourist fish to me." I did not feel like being lunch for the local fishers.

"Well, we're here, and we are tourists. 'When in Rome, do as the Romans do'." she said.

In Rome, Italians spend the mid-day break in the town square, not in small musty bookstores getting ready to purchase a fortune. I was annoyed, but to explain that difference would be pointless. Heather's pleading green eyes told me she'd already made one sacrifice for me today, and now I needed to return the gesture.

Heather headed out with me in tow to find a clerk for the so-called fortune readings. The purchase counter was partially hidden in the dimly lit back of the store. Dust particles floated lazily in the slim strips of light that filtered in through the lowered mini-blinds. Like a trusty hound dog, that once nerve-racking blue line led us to the counter. As Heather rang the service bell, I made note that the same blue line continued past the desk and presumably led to an exit. Maybe it was the flight attendant in me, or the scared rabbit, but knowing my exit brought me great comfort.

We only had to wait a few minutes before we were introduced to Lady Sharone, as she asked us to call her. She entered the room with her head held high, shoulders back, but giving off no airs of callousness. I couldn't help but stare at her. Briefly, she paused to look over some papers. We took that moment to overcome our preconceived ideas of what a woman in her position should look like. By the look on Heather's astonished face, I could tell we both had imagined gypsies from our fairytales. Instead, she was professionally dressed, straight from Saks Fifth Avenue in a loose-fitting tan skirt, black boots, and a snappy white blouse. She only stood at about 5'0" and was stocky with an authoritative persona. Something about her presence immediately put me on my best behavior, in spite of my skepticism. When she spoke, the voice of an angel flowed to our ears. Her words drifted on soft low tones that added to her sophistication.

"Hello, ladies. What is your wish today?" She asked with a smile. We stared back, both of us stunned into silence that did not seem to bother her.

"Hello. We were visiting your town today and noticed your sign out front." Heather spoke first. I nodded in agreement.

Lady Sharone didn't ask which sign, rather she seemed to know. She asked us to follow her into a more private room where we could talk. My once sacrificial act of friendship to follow against my own convictions had taken me to a crossroads. My need to discover why I felt so drawn to her prevailed, and I went willingly.

We entered the back room and arranged ourselves around a small ornate coffee table with characters etched along its side that I could not read. The room was casually decorated with warm green and brown tones. I wondered about her background and why she didn't decorate in the more traditional Victorian colors, keeping in sync with the town's hues of blue and maroon. Soft lighting glowed in the corners of the room, and no round tables with the crystal ball from my fantasy were to be found. Lady Sharone motioned for us to take a seat on a high back couch made out of cedar that had overstuffed cushions for comfort. She was the first to speak as we attempted to settle in for the duration, our bodies sunk into plush mounds. After the day we'd had up to this point, I could have slept there.

"You wish to speak with me?" She said and looked directly at Heather, who got right to the point.

"I'm looking for my purpose, my future I suppose, and I was curious about your offer out front."

"I see," she paused before adding, "To find your purpose is a lifelong journey. However, the opportunity to discover it can always be close."

"I understand foretelling someone's future, but I don't grasp the 'fortunes told and sold' sign out front," said Heather.

Lady Sharone only smiled at her.

"Uh, mostly the 'sold' part," Heather nervously pointed out.

"My dear, one can't buy their fortune like shopping for new clothes, only satisfied until the perfect outfit is found."

She paused to see if we were following her before she continued.

"One may find this foretold future does not follow the fairytale they were dreaming of. Unfortunately I still have to collect my fees even though I 'sold' them a story they did not want to hear," she clarified.

I started to feel the swindle build and could not help but fidget. The couch suddenly was not nearly as comfortable as when I'd first sat down. The madam's gaze left Heather and was now resting on me.

"What is your name, dear?" She asked suddenly.

"Samantha."

Lady Sharone fell silent as if there was more for me to say. I struggled for words as the madam waited for more.

"Uh, my friends call me Sam."

"Samantha. That's a name with an old soul behind it." The madam continued to keep her eyes locked on me as she addressed Heather. "What is yours, dear?"

I slowly nudged Heather, who was unaware she was being spoken to.

"Heather. My friends call me Heather."

I smiled coyly, realizing Heather had spoken my exact words. It's not often my friend was lacking for words of her own. Slowly, the madams' eyes left mine and went to Heather's.

"I see."

Lady Sharone explained that for twenty dollars each, she could help us discover our future. I was well familiar with that look of hopeful curiosity in my friend's eyes. There was no way Heather would walk away now with the key to the unknown dangling right before her. All she had to do was invest twenty dollars and she'd find out how good or how bad her future was destined to be.

I did not believe a word of it. Heather put her money up on the table. I reached into my pocket for twenty dollars and consented to play along. I laid the money next to Heather's, determined to return the same consideration she'd given to me earlier in the day. Heather smiled at what she knew was an effort for me to accept the unacceptable. Lady Sharone interrupted our bonding moment of one for all, all for one.

"There is one warning I will need to share with you." When she felt she had our attention, she continued. "If you're not ready, I cannot help you see your way down any path."

Disappointed, I reached up and took my money off the table. The madam's eyes fell upon me in disapproval, but my main concern was for Heather's feelings. I smiled and extended my arm to indicate the two of them should proceed. Heather's money remained on the table, and I settled back into the couch to watch the show.

Lady Sharone asked Heather if she had anything that was close and personal. She dug around in her purse and pulled out a small flower-etched locket I had never seen before. As Lady Sharone then instructed, Heather obediently closed her eyes, held the locket between the palms of her hands, and began to meditate.

I watched as Lady Sharone glided across the room, well versed in her act. She required only a few moments to dim the lights and spark a few candles. The soft light cascaded our shadows onto the walls behind us, and a smell of vanilla was soon in the air. The mood was now relaxed and tranquil, and I felt my eyes getting heavy from the stress of our day as every cell screamed for some much-needed rest. Enjoying my descent even further into the couch, not willing to terminate this serene feeling, I slipped my hands into my front pockets. My fingertips gently traced my favored souvenir resting there at the bottom. I traced down to its point, where it stung my finger, but I did not recoil. I concentrated on the feel of solid gold as my eyes got heavier. The madam started to lightly sing a song in a language I did not recognize. The last thing I consciously observed through the small slits that were now my eyes was the madam's concentrated gaze. Once again, those eyes settled on me. Her look was intense, but my fatigue was overcoming. The smell of vanilla candles was all around me as I drifted into a dreamland.

I floated for a while in that magical place so many describe when first dozing: that heavy feeling somewhere between consciousness and sleep. I could hear a beeping noise keeping perfect rhythm somewhere within the fog that consumed me. It seemed to beep in sync with the beat of my heart, and it was surprisingly comforting. Along with the rhythmic beat, I could hear muffled conversation in voices I did not recognize. I tried to open my eyes, but found them unwilling, as if someone or something held them shut. I'd never experienced a dream quite like this one. Oddly, I was not scared.

I was startled awake by the sound of a front desk bell that signaled another curiosity seeker had arrived. Sitting upright, I suppressed a yawn and tried not to make it too obvious that I had fallen asleep. Lady Sharone excused herself to tend to the new customer at hand.

"Well, did you find what you were looking for?" I asked Heather, as if I'd been listening all along. Heather watched as I awkwardly held back the need to stretch.

"You couldn't hear for yourself?" Her tone suggested it was not a secret I had been asleep.

"I'm sorry, but she lost me at the 'If your soul is not meant to go that path' crap."

Our conversation was interrupted by our hostess' return. A blush washed over my face as the word 'crap' still seemed to linger in the room. She once again took her seat at the table with Heather.

"I apologize for the delay. Shall we continue?" She asked.

Lady Sharone breathed deeply and lowered her gaze to the tabletop. Time seemed to slow as Heather and I now sat in the uncomfortable silence caused by the dissenting comments we both seemed to wonder if she'd heard. Heather was still clutching the locket when the madam finally looked up.

"Sometimes love is lost for reasons we don't understand." Her unreadable gaze rested on me briefly before turned back to Heather. "Such experiences can either help us grow closer to finding our true purpose or stifle our walk down that path all together. It is in these times when support can be sent from unexpected sources."

Again the madam returned her eyes to me. I fiddled with the hem on the sides of the cushions and pretended not to notice.

"Believe me when I say someone special is coming to help you find your way back onto your righted path."

Heather's eyes lit up. I had seen that look before. Usually it coincided with the appearance of a new man in her life. So, that was it? I couldn't believe men were the most enlightened prediction our hostess could offer. She did not say it would be a man per se, but I considered it was probably easy for Lady Sharone to see we were both still searching for love. Heather took as much joy in the relationship as she did the hunt. I smirked at that fact. Surely this had been what our hostess had easily seen. She told Heather exactly what she wanted to hear. After all, if the relationship did not work out, it would be easy to say he was not meant to be with her on this path of life. I could tell by the wide-eyed look of hope on Heather's face she was hooked with the idea.

"Lady Sharone, exactly when can she expect this person to arrive?" I could not help but push the envelope just a little.

"You'll have to excuse my friend, she's always been a skeptic where people of your profession were concerned."

"If you'll pardon me, I think I will excuse myself. Thank you for your time."

I rose quickly to leave before Heather could protest. Grabbing my oversized handbag, I slipped it over one shoulder and headed for the door. My prediction was that I would say something regrettable if I stayed. Most importantly, I could no longer handle the way our hostess had been inspecting me, as if trying to peer inside my very soul. Truth be known, I had been more afraid of what she might find there if she looked too hard. Though I did not believe this meeting was anything more then a show at the time, there was a sense of aptitude in her eyes when she looked at me. I ignored the possibility that Lady Sharone might have been given some insight. As I exited the room, I nearly upset a massive stack of books. I caught my balance before spilling into a waiting customer.

"Oh," I sputtered as my breath caught in my throat. *Get a grip*, I thought sternly. "Hello. I'm sure my friend will be out soon, and we won't hold you up long."

"Oh, no problem. I'm in no hurry, and she's worth waiting for," answered the woman cheerfully.

"Really? Are you a regular here?" I had to ask.

"Oh, yes. I see her a few times a month. She has been helping me to expand my vision."

Internally I rolled my eyes, but I was brought up to be polite, so I refrained from giving her my thoughts on the matter.

"I see. That must be a great relief to you." I tried to muster up a sincere response, but the stranger's eyes narrowed, and I did not know what to say. "I mean, to see and all, after not being able to see."

I had no idea where I was going, but I was sinking for sure.

"Yes, well it was nice speaking with you." I headed off into the rows of books, regretting I'd responded at all. I looked for a place to hide and wait out my friend's session.

Quite some time later, Heather finally exited Lady Sharone's sanctuary. She found me sitting patiently, a *People* magazine in hand. She bounced on air, uplifted and light on her feet. Her face radiated happiness.

"So, you're good to go then?" I offered, silently hoping we could now leave this place.

"I know you're ready to leave, Sam. I thank you for going along with that for my benefit."

I paused before replying and tried to assess any hint of sarcasm, but found none. I realized how truly happy my friend looked.

"Did she tell you all about the great man you'll meet, and how he'll sweep you off your feet in grand style?" I asked.

Though I was trying to push buttons good naturedly, Heather would not take the bait. She said Lady Sharone was a caring person who truly seemed to know what was in everyone's heart of hearts. Heather told me that though I had not paid, she had spoken to her about me. Lady Sharone had said she felt some deep anger was stifling me. I needed to be moved by the power of love before I could overcome the chains that now bind me.

Her words rang true in my heart. As we left the bookstore, I sensed that something had changed. I couldn't place a finger on it, but the sky seemed a brighter blue as we walked side-by-side back to our hotel. Maybe I did need someone to come along and wake up my heart from its deep slumber. I pushed back tears, wondering how Lady Sharone could have seen what I could not even admit to myself. I decided to rest in the knowledge that she felt someone was coming. Deep down I'd hoped she was right.

DREAM ANGEL

PATRICIA GARBER

CHAPTER ONE

Even through the fog of deep sleep, I sensed his presence in my room. *He's here.* The thought did as much to warm me as did the comforter that covered me. Outside, a bitter midnight chill spread unmercifully across the South. Memphis was gripped by a prevailing winter storm. I imagined sparkling diamonds made of frost blanketing the landscape like a magnificent piece of art.

Though Memphis was far from my Atlanta home, I was nowhere near homesick. Even here in this strange hotel room, I lay as cozy as a baby, my heart fluttering with anticipation, and a smile across my face. "Good things come to patient little girls," an angel had once told me. Since then I had become good at counterfeit patience, hoping to score points for the effort alone.

Maybe tonight was my lucky night?

As an aged wall heater hummed just below the window, the soft and temperate air ruffled around me. Strands of chestnut hair stirred gently over my face as a warm waft passed over me, teasingly carrying his sweet bouquet. Restlessness plagued my body. My mind drifted on a cloud of euphoria, interrupted only when a chair gently creaked.

Soft footsteps approached over the worn carpet, igniting a shiver down my spine. I marveled how a man of his essence could have nearly imperceptible footsteps.

He reached my bedside in three short strides.

I held my breath while butterflies lifted into wild flight patterns inside my stomach, and my heartbeat pulsed inside my ears. My thoughts were scattered, and the minutes passed in torturous anticipation before the bed stirred as he sat down. Ignoring my sham of slumber, he moved closer, and familiar hands shifted under the covers to touch me. His warm silky fingers, caressing me from behind, triggered a firestorm across my skin. My breathing quickly became erratic, and I was shuddering while also melting against his sturdy frame. The warmth from his body was infinitely better than any crackling fire on a bitter winter's day.

"Faker." His soft Mississippi drawl tickled my ear as he nuzzled the nape of my neck. He paused to evaluate my reaction, and then placed a kiss as light as a feather across my bare shoulder.

"You playin' shy now, honey?" He spoke in that butter-melts-in-your-mouth way that always escalated my desire.

Unable to withstand the teasing any longer, I rolled over into his waiting arms. The dark of night failed to hide his iconic features. His high cheek bones, flared nose, and square jaw were visual perfections, but of all his qualities it was his eyes that hypnotized me. Like deep mystic blue pools, they were set ablaze with a rousing fervor I had seen before. I never tired of getting lost in them.

I gathered myself closer and lay my head to his chest with a satisfied moan that mixed with his own exhalation, "I've missed you." I sighed, inhaling his masculine scent deeper into my lungs.

His spicy aroma tantalized my senses. He was as soothing to my spirit as a hot bubble bath, and I never felt happier than when lying in his arms, passing the time in slow, blissful moments of serenity. Too soon, he tenderly pushed me away and looked down into my eyes. I smiled in that bashful way that he enjoyed, and I was rewarded with that famous lopsided grin.

"There's my baby girl."

"Hi." I replied softly.

"Hi, yourself," he chuckled.

"How did you get in here?" I teased.

"I'm an angel, remember?" He grinned and laid his palm against my flushed cheek, skimming his thumb over my mouth.

My lips trembled as he watched me closely, and I knew by his smirk that he was enjoying the eagerness in my eyes. Subconsciously, I wet my lips, and when I thought I could not wait one moment more, his lips were finally on mine.

Instantaneously, I was lost to lips as soft as silk and a kiss as sweet as the richest cream. His mouth was measured and purposeful. He held me where he wanted, and his lips played about mine, a taste here, and a soft touch there. He stirred me slowly, so gently. His every move was calculated perfection, and I melted further into his arms. When he knew our moment was at hand, he shifted his mouth over mine, sinking deeper and enriching our kiss. I opened to him fully, and the salty-sweet taste of him fell to my tongue evoking my moans of pleasure.

A wave of ecstasy swelled. The white-capped waters teeter at the top and promising satisfaction. As my whole body tensed, expecting a flood of delight, his lips suddenly stilled. He pulled back ever so slightly, and the urge to pull him back raged, but I held firm. Through hooded eyes, his gaze smoldered. And, while I licked at his flavor left behind on my lips, his mouth curled in that heart-melting way as he gave me a slow, sly look.

In a single motion, he rolled us as one until I was on my back, and letting out a shriek that was quickly silenced by his mouth crushing down to my own. Where he once was patient he was now demanding. He tugged at me, his kiss varying from fervent to tender and then back again until I was like butter under him. The more I gave, the more he wanted. And, when his practiced hands moved smoothly down my torso to flirt with the soft skin of my inner thigh, I was already whimpering his name into the night.

Mystified, he pulled his lips away.

"Say it again," he whispered a kiss away.

I blinked up in to his smoldering eyes, and even in the dim light I could see him smirking.

"Say it... just once." He raised one dark eyebrow.

I was still breathing heavily, and he kept his pillow-soft lips tantalizingly just above mine. The taste of him lingered on my tongue like a savored treat. My mouth parted for that first syllable of his delicious name, but the second syllable never followed. Without warning, the unwelcoming alarm I had set on my cell phone shrieked from across the room.

Over me, my lover's eyes widened, and, like shattered glass, his perfect features broke in to tiny particles.

I sat straight up in bed so fast that a muscle in my neck cramped with displeasure. I flung my arms outward in a desperate attempt to keep him from leaving, while shielding my eyes as a painfully intense light hit them. I turned to my left and then to my right before plopping backward into the bed with a heavy sigh. Like a ghost in the night, he was gone. The dreams were happening more frequently now, but that didn't mean waking from them was getting any easier.

When the phone shifted from alarm to an actual ring, I leaned across the damp sheets to the bedside table.

"Hello!" I exclaimed breathlessly.

"Samantha?"

"Heather." I inhaled a slow soothing breath.

"Did I interrupt something? You sound breathless."

"No, no I was only... sleeping."

"It sounds as if I caught you doing something far more exciting than sleeping." She chuckled.

"You startled me from a dream, that's all." I yawned.

"Ah, one of *those* dreams." Heather giggled that all-knowing laugh that made me blush, especially when she was right.

"Was there a point to this call?"

"There was, but I've plum forgotten about it now. So, who was he?"

In a flash, I could see Elvis' face smirking over me.

"Nobody."

"Uh-huh. Would that nobody happen to be that famous angel of yours?"

I was silent.

"Sam, he isn't coming back." Heather's voice softened.

My thoughts drifted gently to that unforgettable last evening when my angel revealed that he was a man after all, weak in the flesh, tempted and wanting.

"Samantha Lynn Bennett, are you listening to me?"

I snapped back to attention.

"I know what I should be doing, but yet here I am."

"Exactly. Why are you in Memphis?"

"It's his birthday." I was beginning to regret having shared my destination on her voice mail before I left Atlanta yesterday morning.

"He doesn't celebrate birthdays anymore, Samantha. He's dead."

The shock value of "dead" slowly sunk in.

"I needed to be near him. Look… I have to go. I'm late to meet Steve." I hung up on her abruptly and wished I hadn't.

Heather knew nothing about Steve. In fact, I knew very little about him myself. The way we met was unexpected and could have been a scene straight out of a Nora Ephron movie. But, I was no Meg Ryan, and I wasn't looking for the likes of Tom Hanks. I wanted my angel, and I knew where to find him.

My first stop when I arrived in Memphis was Graceland, to pay my respects. After all, the date was January 8, where else would I be? It was nighttime and unbelievably cold, too cold to be outside, but there we were the last two die-hard fans of the day to leave the estate. Even though we only spoke briefly through chattering teeth, something about him intrigued me. We shared a warming cup of coco that night, and without hesitation, I accepted his invitation to meet for morning coffee.

On one hand, I looked forward to a friendly face, someone who understood my love for a man I had never met. Or so Steve assumed. Another part of me, my much less confident side, hoped a certain angel would be watching.

How does one attract an angel's attention? Since his departure from my life, this question had been haunting every hour of my day. I could find no definitive answer. There were no written instructions for me to follow, and the Bible spoke sparingly of such things. I found myself relying on my own humanistic ideas which, of course, meant my plan was flawed from the start.

* * *

With only thirty minutes before I was to meet Steve at the café across from Graceland, I jumped into the shower and raced to get ready. The legacy of my childhood upbringing to literally and unfailingly be at church on time was that as an adult, I could not tolerate lateness. As I rushed about the room like a madwoman, trying not to be haphazard and waste the little time I had, my cell phone insistently rang with the sound of "Treat Me Nice."

Heather was persistent, I'd give her that. I would have explained my plans to her, but she would only worry. I let the first, second and third calls all go to voice mail.

Racing the clock, I made a mental note to change my ring tone to something more reflective of my current mood. I considered "Hurt," and then just as quickly tossed that idea aside. "The Sound of Your Cry" popped in to my mind. Better? No, the song I had was upbeat, and I could use all the help I could get.

I loved my angel. Was that not an acceptable excuse for chasing after him? After all, it was he who so abruptly left me, confused and literally alone in a bed smelling of his savory cologne. And, I wasn't the type of woman who took men to her bed, even if they were Elvis Presley. I prided myself in being a good girl. Now, who was I? If God would only tell me how this was all supposed to work, this loving of angels, my life would be much easier. But so far, God wasn't speaking. Or maybe it was I that was not listening? Nothing was clear.

What if God was silent for a reason? My mind spun around that question like a caged hamster on its wheel. Did he expect me to let Elvis go after all we've been through? Even the words "letting go" felt as thick on my tongue as a mouthful of cotton. No, I defiantly shook my head at nobody in particular. It wasn't time to let go. Not yet.

In two fluid and familiar movements, I unpinned my long chestnut hair and quickly tied it back into the default time-saver: a ponytail. I paused to look at my reflection in the mirror. My oval features and defined cheek bones were hauntingly familiar, a walking reflection of my mother. And upon looking closer, my blue eyes sparkled with a new look, one of death-defying determination. This woman before me, throwing caution to the wind, was such a stranger to me the mere sight of her stopped me in my own tracks.

I reached for my purse, wondering if it was a sin to want what God himself had given me. While nibbling nervously on my bottom lip, I suddenly smiled. No, I won't think of it today. Happily, I decided to side with Scarlett O'Hara.